FINDING MOKSHA

One Woman's Path in Uncertain Times

D1568778

— Amanda L. Mottorn —

ISBN: 9798587356177 (paperback)

Dedicated to survivors and in memory of those who could not.

~ 1 ~

Dad opened and closed the cabinet door under the sink by the table. "Have you seen my Merlot?"

"No." Mom rinsed and stacked dinner dishes in the dishwasher.

I couldn't see the two of them from my living room chair. I held my breath, looked up from the book of Robert Frost poetry in my lap.

Beneath the sink, the sound of the cabinet door opened, then closed. Twice. It always stuck and was louder the second time.

"I bought more."

"I don't know where it is." Mom's voice was soft behind the running water.

Dad's heavy steps went down the stairs.

I walked into the kitchen and sat in my chair by the sink. I couldn't help smiling.

Mom looked focused in her cleaning, though we met eyes.

The decorative jingle bells of the door clanged. It led to the garage where the storage room was. After a few minutes, he was back in the house. My shoulders rose. The sound of Dad's leather shoes moved on the stone floor toward his office.

"I know what you're doing." Mom's low voice was to my back.

I turned around. "I don't know what you're talking about."

"You hid his wine. Get it and put it back. He'll go back to the store and buy more. We shouldn't waste money."

The fight drained out of me. I took long breaths to control my hot anger from slipping. I turned around and marched downstairs to the garage. The door closed without a sound. Opening the closet surrounding the furnace, I leaned against the white wall fighting back tears that came, wiped them away and leaned over, picking up the jug, wanting to smash it against the white wall with red liquid spilling everywhere. My arm circled the bottle and I carried it on my hip. The closet door closed behind me and I walked up the steps. Without the sound of the bells, the door opened and shut. Dad's TV blared from his office.

Avoiding Mom's eyes, I opened the cabinet and pushed the jug on the shelf to the farther side. The shelf always had a new bottle or a partially drunk one in addition to Mom's diet pops.

Her eyes met mine as I whacked the cabinet shut. My throat tightened.

Dad came into the room. "Evie, get out of the way. I need to get under there."

"Nothing is left." I lied and moved to look out the windows as night fell upon our big backyard.

Like the sound of sand paper, pop bottles moved on

the lower shelf and the glass was shifted from the far side. It would be awkward to reach, but Dad's arms were long.

He sighed.

I turned to him.

"What's the matter with you?"

I shrugged and looked back to the window. Dad carried the bottle out of the kitchen and downstairs to his office. I leaned my elbow on the white and black marble ledge.

I turned to go downstairs. We were watching a movie after dinner.

"Evie, wait a minute." Mom turned from the sink.

"What?" I glared.

"This is a family matter. It's no one's business." Mom's eyes searched mine.

I didn't say anything.

"Promise you won't talk about your dad's drinking to anyone."

I stared at her, my jaw clenched.

"Promise," she repeated.

"Fine. I promise."

She nodded.

Walking away, I turned around. "Why do you let him drink?"

She looked at me a long time. Her eyes were cloudy like an old person's.

"Because I can't take care of you kids on my teaching salary. Growing up poor is no way to live."

"But it's okay to have an alcoholic father."

"He's not that. He functions."

"You're blind."

"You'll understand when you're older."

"What about when he promised to help you with your certification that one night? Except the bar called you to pick him up at two in the morning because he had too much."

"There are things you don't know. Without your dad, you wouldn't have art classes or piano lessons. Remember all those clothes I bought you? Imagine not having those things. It's no life without money."

I looked at her, turned and went down the stairs. I put the comforter over me. The fire needed another log and I got up and poked around the fireplace. I turned on the TV waiting for Mom to finish the dishes. Then I went into Dad's office to get him so we could start the movie.

The room was dimly lit with the brown and white stained glass covering the light. The brick laminate cooled my bare feet. On one wall were wooden shelves with sliding doors on the lower half for storage. Drawers with iron handles held tossed in papers. The counter above the drawers was covered with Dad's binders. On his desk were computer wires, textbooks and pliers.

To the left, in the corner Dad's computer sat at an angle. Above the desk the painting with a scene from the Middle Ages hung.

"Dad?"

The crackled gold wine goblet was nearly empty and the jug wine sat on the corner of the desk.

"What?" Dad's chair squeaked as he turned.

"We're waiting for you to watch the movie."

Dad took another gulp of his red wine, finishing it. He turned to pour another glass to the top. "I have things to do."

"But you promised. It's a weekend night."

"Not tonight."

"Come on, Dad." I put my hands on the back of his chair.

He shook his head and stared ahead at the white TV on the shelf. Some history program droned on.

I sighed and walked out. Mom saw my hunched shoulders as I rounded the corner for the family room. Her forehead creased.

"Dad's not coming."

I watched the darkness pass Mom's face.

She pushed play on the VCR remote aimed toward the TV. I went back to the couch under the blanket. Mom's eyes burned on me but I refused to acknowledge her. I pushed disappointment down into my chest.

That night I woke up in the middle of the night, having gone to bed after the movie. Mom had gone upstairs hours ago. I heard a bumping noise. My arm hairs went up. Then I heard the downstairs hall ceiling lamp move; sometimes Dad knocked his head on it when he wasn't paying attention. I tip-toed down the hall and the steps, avoiding creaking floorboards.

He leaned against the closet, grabbing on to it.

"Dad, are you okay?" I hissed.

He looked up at me, a smile on his face. "Evie, you think you can get your ol' dad up the steps?"

My voice rose. "Should I get Mom?"

"You're already here."

I looked into his office and saw the empty wine jug.

Dad shifted.

"How can you do this?"

"You sound like your mother." Dad's smile faded as he took a couple steps and leaned on the iron railing. I stood and put my arm around him.

I turned my head away smelling the alcohol. "You better sleep on the couch in the living room; you'll never make it up to the bedroom."

"No confidence in your old man, huh." Dad chuckled and started to sing.

"Shh. You'll wake up Mom."

The walk up the five steps in our split-level house was awkward. Dad was tall and broad and I hadn't reached my full height yet. When we made it to the top, a step at a time, Dad sat on the rust colored plaid couch. I walked to the kitchen and filled up a glass of water for Dad. When I came back in the living room carrying the glass, Dad stood in a corner like a dog against a tree. I forgot about being quiet. "Dad! This is the living room!"

He turned around his head. The sound of pee hit the side of the fireplace.

I dropped the glass and it broke into pieces around my bare feet.

He shook his head like he woke up. "Evie, don't move." He slurred. "I'm going to help."

I heard him zip and button his jeans. He leaned on the wall for support and turned around to stagger toward me.

"Get away from me. And don't ever talk to me about this." I took a big leap toward the kitchen and put on my slippers from downstairs.

Dad was sleeping on a chair by the time I came back up.

I swept up all the glass and then followed it with a wet paper towel.

~ 2 ~

Two months later on a Saturday afternoon, Mom was vacuuming the house.

"Your dad can drop you off at the Giant Eagle. I need shortening and flour for the pie crust. Don't forget the lemons. I need fresh ones, not that bottled kind."

"What are you making?"

"It's for lemon meringue pie while your sister's home this weekend; she'll be arriving any minute." Mom smiled.

"Can't we have key lime? I hate that fluffy meringue."

Mom gave me the look and I kept my mouth shut. Lemon meringue was Elizabeth's and Mom's favorite.

Sitting on the plush navy seats of the blue Park Avenue, I pushed the button for the windows to go down as Dad pulled out of the driveway. "What errands do you have?"

"I need to mail some things for clients. I'm stopping at the American Legion for a beer while you get your mother's groceries."

I sighed.

"The grocery store will be busy. It's a Saturday. People will be getting chips and pretzels for the Steeler game tonight." His voice snapped.

I looked out the window watching the dense green maple and oak trees go by. I bent into my open window. "Don't forget to pick me up."

Dad waved his hand. "I'll be back in thirty minutes."

I watched Dad pull away from the Eagle and went inside. Dad was right; it was busy.

After getting the items on the list, I went back out in front of the store and sat on the green bench with five minutes to wait. The bench was hot on my legs. People came and went leaving with their grocery carts of filled brown paper bags. I shifted my weight trying to get comfortable. My stomach gurgled; Dad would be here any minute. I sat up straighter.

Cars drove by. After a while I stood up to stretch. I took the change out of my pocket wondering if I should call Mom but she'd be busy cooking dinner. I looked down at my watch. Dad gets a ten minute grace period. I started pacing. Picking up the grocery bag, I walked around the corner and scanned the parking lot. I walked back to the bench and stood by it looking further to the other side of the lot. My jaw clamped down. I sat again and pulled my knees into my chest. He was now fifteen minutes late.

We ate at 6:00, exactly then, because Dad started arguing with Mom if dinner wasn't ready. I sat back down on the bench and put my chin in my hands. My bony elbows dug into my knees.

I looked up, hearing a familiar older woman's voice call my name.

"Eva."

I stood up. It was Mrs. Jones, our retired widowed neighbor from across the lawn.

"What are you doing, dear?"

"Waiting for my dad to pick me up. He's late."

Mrs. Jones' lips became a thin line.

"I'm sure he'll be here any minute." I brightened.

"If he isn't here when I finish shopping, I'll run you home."

"He'll be here."

She nodded; her smile returned and she patted my arm.

I looked into the grocery bag.

Cars came and went and shoppers I'd seen gone in were coming out again. Some looked at me, but I stared straight ahead at the highway in front of the parking lot.

Mrs. Jones came back out; I was focusing on the ground. My fists clenched against the sides of my legs.

"Eva, I'll run you home."

I stood up with all the energy I had.

"Put your bag in the cart with mine."

I put it in, glad for a task.

We loaded Mrs. Jones' cranberry Plymouth Volare, with the horizontal striped seats.

"I'll take the cart back," I said.

"Thanks, dear."

I walked the cart back wondering if Dad was going to show up now and he better not because I didn't want to lie to Mrs. Jones about why Dad was late. I got into the car as she turned the key in the ignition. The drive home was slow, partly because Mrs. Jones didn't drive the speed limit. She asked me about what kids my age were learning in tenth grade. It helped me keep back the tears of Dad forgetting me. After thanking her and helping her bring in her groceries, I took long strides across the lawn home.

I walked in the house carrying the bag of groceries and dropped them on the counter in front of where Mom stood.

"Where's your dad?"

I shrugged. "American Legion?"

"Who brought you home?"

"Mrs. Jones happened to be at Giant Eagle."

"I waited for Dad a long time." My voice raised.

Mom's eyebrows slanted and the lines in her forehead deepened. Her voice was low. "Dinner is ready. Call your sister."

I walked a few feet to the stairs and called Elizabeth.

She hollered back. "I'll be down in a minute."

I went to sit at my chair.

Mom wasn't saying anything but her eyebrows knitted together as she picked up the phone and stood by the microwave.

"What are you doing?" I asked.

"Hi, Nell; thank you for picking up Evie and bringing her home. Ed must've been held up in traffic."

Then it was quiet. Mom said a few other things and hung up.

My sister walked into the kitchen.

"Elizabeth, put the hot pad down for the meatloaf."

The microwave beeped and the succotash came out. Mom banged the pot taking the beaters out and spooning potato remnants off. She gave one to each of us to lick like she did with chocolate desserts. I ran my fingers over it getting every last bit of the buttery potatoes. I put the cleaned beater in the sink in the pan now filled with water. We sat down.

"Even if your father can't be on time, it doesn't mean we have to let the food get cold."

She picked up her fork and ate the meatloaf.

I made a puddle in my mashed potatoes and put in a slice of butter, pouring gravy on top. Elizabeth started to eat and we talked like a normal family, passing plates and serving up another slice of meatloaf.

"This is good, Mom," Elizabeth and I echoed.

"Thanks, girls." Mom's lips upturned, the tightness gone from her forehead.

Everyone stopped eating when we heard the garage door open.

"Keep eating."

Elizabeth and I looked at each other, then down at our plates.

Dad opened the door from the garage to the family room, the bell jangling as it shut with a slam.

Dad was singing one of his old Scottish drinking songs. We heard him go to the foyer and kick off his loafers. He walked up the stairs to the kitchen.

"Sorry I'm late. I saw someone I knew. And I brought

fish home from Zackle's. Here." He stretched out his hand toward Mom, waiting for her to stand.

Mom remained in her chair. She kept eating her meatloaf.

Elizabeth and I looked at each other. My stomach knotted as a burning in my throat came up.

My chair screeched back on the floor as I stood up. "You were supposed to pick me up. I waited almost an hour. I'd probably still be there if Mrs. Jones hadn't gone shopping. You promised you wouldn't forget me." I crossed my arms and then re-crossed them.

Dad didn't answer, avoided my eyes and put the bag of fish on the counter.

Mom stood up. "I asked you to drop off Evie to get ingredients for the pie tomorrow."

"You need to take better care of the kids. If you can't do everything, I should hire a maid. Or, you need to quit that teaching job."

Mom opened the cabinet and took out a plate and silverware for Dad. She slammed the cabinet back. "Dinner's getting cold." She yelled. "We depend on you to help out. Evie waited for you and so did Elizabeth and me. I had to lie to Nell again that you were stuck in traffic. You knew I was making your favorite dinner tonight."

Mom looked at me. Her voice softened. "Evie, sit back down."

I swallowed hard holding back tears and sat with the chair still pushed back.

Dad sat and was quiet a long minute. "Elizabeth, pass me the meatloaf."

— 3 —

Every spring and summer we went to Cook Forest State Park a couple hours' drive from our house; the Clarion River runs through old growth hemlocks.

After parking the car by the pond where kids and their fathers fished, we started zig-zagging up to the trails leading to the old growth forest, rare in Pennsylvania from extensive logging in the nineteenth century. It was a short hike but I loved nothing more than to marvel and hike in the dense trees smelling the fresh pine. Maple, beech and oak leaves, dirt and rocks were underfoot large boulders in the middle of the pine covered floor. As we crossed the bridge and walked past the creek, we returned to the parking lot.

Dad talked to the canoe rental man and paid a fee to carry our aluminum canoe and a rented one for Mom and me. The man drove the road full of potholes as fast as he could up ten miles of the river. I shared glances with Mom, wondering if our canoes would remain attached to the trailer. We held on tight to the seat back in front of us bumping up and down in the van. There were no seatbelts. Hot July air blew at us from the opened windows as my hair flew in every direction.

When the death trap ride stopped, we filed out one after the other, putting our boats in the water, the orange life vests sitting in the bottom of the boats. Sometimes we used them for extra cushions.

Dad waited for Mom and me to sit in the rented canoe and pushed us out into the river. I was in the back and Mom's job was to paddle and help me look out for rocks. The current would take us back to the parking lot by the end of the day.

Dad steadied the canoe that my parents bought before Elizabeth was born and helped her into the front. The canoe had fabric orange plaid seats over an aluminum bench. Dad made sure the cooler with our lunches and snacks was square and stable in the middle of the boat. He walked it out further and sat on the seat.

I paddled in the back, the steering function, as we always sat.

Mom shouted, "To the left."

I paddled; turning was slow.

"A rock up ahead, Eva."

"Okay."

I did a furious stroke and the boat moved. The current pulled us downstream. Dense forest surrounded us on the river. I lifted my paddle out of the boat and sat back, feeling the sun hitting my face, and re-adjusted my hat as I lay back. I watched Mom paddle, amused that she didn't know she was doing all the work. The silver canoe holding Dad and Elizabeth raced into my line of vision. They passed us and canoed on the right in a straight line coming up to the old weeping willow on a shore where children played. We zig-zagged to catch up, Mom shouting instructions.

"To the right, Eva."

I paddled some, trying to straighten us out.

"To the left, a rock is up ahead."

I watched whirlpools form as my oar moved back and the boat carried us down to catch up with Dad and Elizabeth. Mom and I paddled together, almost going in a straight line at a fast pace.

"Way to go, Mom," I hollered.

She switched sides and the boat turned. I switched and we paddled more of the river than most boaters.

"That's it, Eve," Mom shouted when we were straight again.

I smiled. Sweat formed above my lip. Despite the work, my shoulders relaxed as I took in the woods around us and listened to the sounds of the water, birds chirping and flying overhead and nestled in the trees. Children shouted and laughed on the passing shores. Our boats joined together.

"It's beautiful." I looked to Dad.

He nodded.

"Hand me a diet coke, Elizabeth."

She opened the mustard yellow cooler and took out a can and handed it to Mom.

Elizabeth looked to me. "Want anything?"

"No, I have my thermos."

Elizabeth removed a diet pop for herself and opened the can.

We paddled down the river. Soon it was time for lunch and we scouted for a boulder that wasn't already taken. We found one with room for pulling off both boats sandwiched between rocks. After mooring the boat, Dad tested the depth with his paddle and jumped out, the water up to his knees. He gave Elizabeth a hand in stepping out. Then he waited for Mom to approach still in our boat, and helped her in getting out. He brought her in closer and gave her a kiss.

Elizabeth and I exchanged looks.

"You're embarrassing," I said.

Returning my gaze to my sister, she smiled back and shrugged.

After we were all settled on the rock, Mom handed out designated sandwiches with first letters for each of our names. Elizabeth had the peanut butter, banana, pickle hoagie roll. I had the ham, cheese, and tomato. Dad had everything on his and Mom had something between mine and Dad's.

We ate our lunches our legs stretched out like Dad's.

"Pass the chips," Elizabeth said. Dad gave her the chips, stopping at Mom.

"I'm taking my foldovers," Mom fished out the crunchiest ones, the chips that were baked folding over. After taking a handful, she passed the bag to Elizabeth.

After lunch we ate brownies Mom had made while my sister and I were sleeping that morning. She added mint chocolate candies for a melted topping, my favorite.

Our bellies full, we climbed back into our boats with

Dad's help, making sure we were settled before pushing us off. We paddled down the river, our chatter light and full of laughs.

I moved our boat closer to Dad's and Elizabeth. "Let's sing a round."

You have to stay on your part," Dad pointed at me and chuckled.

"I always do."

My sister glared at me. "Right."

Elizabeth and Mom sang like they belonged in a chorus; Dad was the tenor we needed. My singing was flat and off-key; Dad always said enthusiasm counts, and so I was.

Dad called it "the paddling song,"
Our paddles keen and bright,
Flashing like silver;
Swift as the wild goose flight,
Dip, dip and swing."

— 4 —

On a Saturday afternoon I was at home reading in the Colonial blue chair in the living room. Elizabeth was at college and Mom was out grocery shopping.

The phone rang.

I ran to pick it up, my book dropping on the floor. "Hello?"

Dad's words came out slow, blurred at the ends.

"Dad?"

"You need to pick me up."

"Are you okay?"

The line was quiet. "I can't drive. Come get me at the Italian Club."

"That's a four mile walk. It'll be awhile before I get there. I only have my learner's permit. Mom's not home."

"Don't tell your mother about this."

Putting on my socks and shoes, I walked down our street and the adjacent one toward the grassy side of Route 65 as cars whizzed by. My pace was faster than usual. I hoped Dad could walk by himself. The summer day was long before dusk would come.

Upon arriving at the parking lot lined by a couple telephone poles, I noted Dad's white pick-up truck had a new indentation in the back. As I walked into the wood paneled bar from floor to ceiling, a strong cigarette smell entered my nose. Dad sat on one of the black vinyl stools lining the bar.

"What happened to your truck?"

"I didn't see the pole."

A half finished beer sat on the bar next to Dad. He took another swig.

I looked at him not understanding why he kept drinking.

Dad looked back at the bartender and pursed his lips.

The bartender handed me the keys, meeting my eyes. He looked past me toward the entrance as someone came in.

I faced Dad. "I haven't driven at night. How are you going to help me?" My voice rose.

Dad stood on his own, one hand on the bar for support. "Stop worrying; you're like your mother."

-5-

In the fall muffled shouting came through the walls in my room. I put down my book for my eleventh grade class, stood up and opened the door, avoiding the squeak. Sucking in my belly and stepping sideways out of my room, I walked closer down the hall, the braided rug warming my feet.

"I'm not paying for art school. She'll end up unemployed." Dad's voice was loud down two levels in the foyer outside his den.

"The art classes are important to her. Carnegie Mellon doesn't choose untalented students."

"I'm not spending any of my hard-earned money for her to be jobless. She needs to learn what pays the bills."

"She had to pass a prerequisite course to take the painting class. She has talent."

"No more classes at that university."

"It's enough what you do to me, saying you'll help out with this two acre yard you said you wanted, only to be in here drinking another jug of wine instead. I have plenty to do taking care of the girls, my job and this house."

"I told you to keep your job as long as it didn't interfere with your house duties. Maybe you should quit."

It sounded like Mom threw one of Dad's computer manuals against the wall.

Dad's wooden chair screeched. "Look what you did."

"Why can't Eva be more like Elizabeth? We'll never have to worry about her. Tell Eva she's quitting. You should resign from your job. I told you a woman's place belongs in the home. I can't believe I let you get away with working."

I had heard Dad threaten her many times before. I knew how much Mom's job meant. Her job kept bills paid when Dad was laid off.

I would never have Elizabeth's business sense. Solving math problems came easily for her; art classes were free-ing. I could paint or draw and get lost in the color and the brush strokes. There were no arguing parents. There were smiles, laughter and encouraging teachers.

"Edward, you can't do this to her. It isn't right."

"Women have three work choices. Teacher, nurse, li-brarian. Elizabeth is heading in the right direction dating that football player. She'll make a fine teacher."

"The girls need to follow their own direction. Evie should continue with her art and build her skills; she can teach. How can you keep her from doing what she loves? She's a child, Edward."

"Enough." My dad's terse finality hung in the air.

Silence filled the house and then the sound of Mom's wedding ring hit the iron railing, and fast steps ran up the hardwood floors to the living room and into the kitchen. I ducked into another bedroom. The oven door slammed even though nothing was cooking at 9:00 at night.

I went back to my room and picked up my Ernest Hemingway book of short stories. After twenty minutes of reading the same paragraph, I went downstairs to find Mom on a chair in the living room reading a Dick Francis mystery novel.

"Mom?"

She looked up from her book and put the library card in to keep her place.

"Yes?"

"I'm going to be able to keep taking art classes, right?"

Her eyebrows furrowed and her stress lines returned.

I looked back to where Dad's office was, the door closed.

"He can't hear you."

She stood up from the chair and put her hands on her hips. "Not at Carnegie Mellon."

I folded my arms into my chest. The old familiar ache in my shoulders increased. "I heard. Why didn't you tell him it will look better on my college applications? All the art schools have started sending me their forms."

She cupped my shoulders. "He won't pay for it. Tell you what, we'll go shopping tomorrow. We'll have a girls' day, just you and me."

"I don't want a shopping trip. I want the art classes." I shook away from her. "I can try to pay for that painting class. My part-time job at the library will never earn me enough; maybe I can get more hours. I'll never get another scholarship; that was for first timers and I had to do the prerequisite."

"You can't work any more hours. You had a C in geometry. Your dad wanted you to quit your job, but I told him it would teach you about saving and finance. It's the only reason he agreed."

"That teacher stinks and never used the chalkboard. He explained everything by drawing in the air. What an idiot. I wasn't the only one with a bad grade."

"That's not how your dad sees it."

I slumped my shoulders, sighed and blew a piece of hair out of my face.

"You'll have to settle for community college classes. Your art has to be a hobby from now on. You'll need to support yourself until you find a husband. You can't make it on your own, especially as a woman."

"You said you wanted to help." I stepped back.

"Your dad won't see any other way." Avoiding my eyes, she walked away and sat on the couch. She leaned over and started straightening the coffee table's piles of newspapers and magazines.

I couldn't stop the tears from coming. "How can you do this?"

Her eyes remained down on the table. "You know how your dad is. Once he makes up his mind, there's no changing it."

"Can't you wait until he gets drunk, make it so he gets confused and says yes?"

She looked up at me. "He won't pay for this."

I stepped toward her towering above, only the coffee table separating us. "You're taking away what matters most."

"You can take classes at community college."

"You let him walk all over you and now it's me."

She stood up to face me, wrinkle lines of anger pronounced in her face. Her voice was a loud and fast whisper. "Stop it. Your art can never matter."

Pain rose in my chest. Tears fell from my face.

Mom walked around the coffee table to hug me.

My arms remained at my sides. Maybe Dad even thought I was worthless.

"It'll be okay." She rubbed my back.

"Tomorrow we'll have a wonderful time together." She took my hand in hers. "I know it hurts."

I nodded, wiped away my tears and let her hug me.

~6~

"I can't believe you read my diary."

"You shouldn't be doing that with Chris. Your dad was right to keep you from those classes. You're supposed to wait until marriage. You'll get a reputation." She slammed the long pantry cabinet and turned to face me.

The old familiar ache returned to my shoulders. "You don't know anything."

"You don't talk to me." She walked to the sink, turned on the water and rinsed the utensils before piling them on the counter.

"My diary is private."

She leaned down on the counter and pointed at me. "While you live in this house, nothing is a secret. I hope Chris is the only one."

"The only what?!" I put my hands out on the table, each finger spread out.

"The only boy you're doing that with."

"You don't even know what you're talking about."

"The hell I do. I was young once and I didn't do what you did until I was married. I'm ashamed of you." Mom picked up the pewter napkin holder and slammed it on the laminate counter between us.

"When Chris has dinner, his parents hold hands during prayer. When do you and Dad hold hands anymore?!"

"How dare you use that language with me. What your dad and I do is our business. And you're grounded. You'll be lucky to go out with your friends for the next month. You will not see him again."

I stood up so her eyes moved to my height. "You can't make me stop."

"I know what's best for you."

"You know nothing."

"Look at all those new clothes in your closet." Mom looked down picking up a bowl from the counter and wiped away yogurt in the running water.

I put my hands on my hips and stood taller.

She stepped close to me even with the sink between us and squinted her eyes.

I took a big step away, my hands toward my sides, palms up, fingers spread.

She stayed bolted in her position. "Until you learn about respect, you'll stay grounded. If you don't go out, you'll have more study time. Don't you want to get into a good college? You can meet your husband there."

I clenched my jaw.

"I didn't want to read your diary, but you stopped talking to me." She reached toward me.

I stepped back. "You and Dad made me quit my art. You two aren't like any of my friends' parents."

"I said you could take art classes at community college."

"Everyone's at least sixty-five!"

The furrowed lines left Mom's face.

"I had to tell my friends that Dad said I would end up unemployed. It was humiliating."

"You'll understand when you're older with your own kids." She walked around the corner, stepping toward me.

I thrust my hands in my jeans pockets. "I'm not having a family."

"You don't know what you're talking about. A woman's role is to have children. How would you like it if I said that about you?" Her voice softened as she put her hands on my wrists.

I wiggled off her loose grasp. "I'd say, good, because you'd be choosing what you wanted." I turned away to get a glass out of the cabinet and went to the sink.

She stood where I'd left her, my back still turned to her.

"You're a young lady. You don't want boys to think you're easy. If you think your life is bad now, it'll be worse because you'll end up pregnant."

I turned to face her.

Her arms were crossed hard against her chest.

"For god's sakes, I'm not pregnant. And I'd have an abortion even if I was."

She sighed. "If you ended up pregnant, you'd have that baby. Only in cases when the mother is in danger or raped would you be permitted to have an abortion."

"It's almost 1990; this isn't the 1950s."

She raised her voice, speaking with fast staccato words. "You will not go out for the rest of the school year."

I looked down at her and squinted my eyes.

"You'll understand when you're older." She turned away, opening the fridge and looked inside a long time.

I stared at her feet in her wool slipper socks that she'd started wearing to hide her knotted arthritic toes. Dad thought it was funny to say he was married to part-woman, part alien.

"I don't have to be miserable like you and Dad. I've grown up watching you hate each other."

She turned and slammed the refrigerator door. "I can't believe you'd say such horrible things."

I walked over to the table and shoved a chair.

She turned to me and stepped close. "Now what did I say about respect, young lady?"

I didn't move except to keep towering over her. "Respect: That means letting Dad walk all over the three of us? And hearing you repeat Dad's wishes so Elizabeth and I are put down? Respect: pretend nothing bad is happening, stuffing it deep down so we can be rewarded with shopping trips."

The lines returned to Mom's forehead. Her blue veined hands leaned on the table. "That mouth of yours is out of control. You'll be lucky if you ever see the outside of these four walls. No more piano lessons. No more art supplies. You're on your own." She stepped away opening the pantry door, looking hard in the empty spaces between canned beans and boxes of rice.

~7~

School was almost over that year but I was still grounded.

I almost jumped from the sound of the phone. I was packing my things into a duffle bag.

Mom hollered, "Evie, it's for you."

I shoved the clothes in the bag and under the bed; I hollered through the closed door.

"Who is it?"

"Your cousin Michelle."

I surveyed my room making sure nothing looked amiss. I reached for the phone and sat on the corner of my bed.

"Hi, Shel."

"What's wrong?"

"Nothing." I put the phone on my ears and looked at my list of what else I needed to pack.

"How are you?" My voice was higher than I meant.

"Everything's fine."

"Eva, what happened?"

The line was quiet.

My throat burned. I blinked hard. "I said. nothing."

"Eva, tell me what's going on. I know something's not right."

I stood up and walked to the window where the weeping willow was. "It's too hard with my parents. I can't take it anymore. I'm packing."

"What? To go where?"

"There's an abandoned house nearby. I'll stay there for now. I've got my sleeping bag and some clothes packed."

"It's tough with your parents but you can't run away. This doesn't even make sense. You don't know how to live on your own. You can't stay in a place like that; you can't do this, Evie. It's a really bad idea."

I bit my nail. My jaw hurt. "I can't deal with hiding my dad's drinking. And I hate how he puts down my mom and us; she covers for him anyway."

"Evie, yes, it's very hard, but if you leave now, you're giving up any good future you could have. You have to stay there. Your parents love you."

"How can you say that?"

"I know it's hard. But you've got to finish school. Your dad will pay for college and then you'll be free."

I tore off a nail and my skin burned. It started to bleed and I reached for the tissue box. "How do you expect me to deal with all this in the meantime? It's easy for you. You're not here."

"I wish I was there. You've got to stay put. It's not easy being on your own. I made it to college. I see the bills and what it costs. My parents are paying for all of my expenses until I graduate. It costs a lot of money to live. The apartment rate, the heating, the electricity.

You can't live in an abandoned house. You need to be safe."

"I can't take this anymore."

"Don't look at it like that. Look at it as day by day. You'll have a good future by staying there. It's not bad every single day, right? Just sometimes, it's tough."

I closed my eyes. "Yes." I moved away from the window and sat on the corner of my bed, crossing my legs.

"Suppose you did run away. What would you do for food? Where would you stay that would be safe? What if something bad happened? Evie, I know it is hard now but if you ran away, it won't make anything better. It would be much worse. And not even have a high school diploma. Who would hire you not having a place of residence?"

I stayed silent.

"Your parents provide a warm and safe place. You've got to finish school. Even getting to college will give you a taste of what it's like to be on your own. And then you can make the big decisions about where you'll live."

"Hmm."

"Are you listening?"

"Yes."

"Do you trust me?"

"More than anyone else in the world."

Shel sighed. "Then trust me on this. I know what I'm talking about from living in this apartment and seeing the monthly bills. If it wasn't for my parents paying, I don't know how I would do it."

"Right." My voice felt small.

"Look, it's summer time. You have more time to paint. You can hike with your dad sometimes. It's hard to see the positives in all this; I know. I wish I could make your dad stop drinking. But I can't."

"Mmmm."

"Promise me you'll forget about running away. Say it out loud."

"I promise I won't run away." My voice was low in case my mother was listening through the door.

"And what else?"

"I'll stay in high school and somehow deal with this. Dad will pay for college and then I'll be free."

"Good."

I clutched the phone to my ear and moved my hand releasing my cramped fingers.

Tears formed in my eyes. "You always call when I need you. How do you know?"

"You're my kid sister, Evie, even though we're cousins. I love you." Her voice brightened and I could hear her smile.

My throat tightened. "I love you, too. I don't know what I'd do without you."

"You'll never be without me."

"You're my favorite Shelley-Belly."

"Stop calling me that — between you and my dad!"

"Come on, you like it. Uncle Jack told me."

I didn't mention her younger brother Rory; they were always fighting. Jess, Michelle's older sister was already out of the house.

"You and my dad have to stop it."

"Stop crossing your arms. You're causing welts."

"Who said I was doing that?"

"I know you."

She paused.

"How's college going?"

"Almost finished. It's great."

"You'll be a cool reporter." I moved the pillows against the headboard and leaned back.

"Let's hope so."

"How's your boyfriend?" I pulled my knees into my chest.

"Mark? He's good; he'll be a horse veterinarian."

"He'll be in school forever."

"I know."

"What happens when you graduate?"

"When I get a job at a newspaper, we'll move in together."

"Your life is all working out. I want to be just like you."

"It isn't as easy as it sounds. You have to work hard in high school. Then the same in college and somehow balance it out between studying, friends and all that."

"It sounds like a dream."

"It'll be reality in no time, I promise."

"I hope so. My mom says it isn't right that you're paying Mark's bills with your waitressing tips since you have the job. But she's old school."

"My parents don't like it either. It's my life, not theirs. I don't need much; Mark had a hard upbringing. Rory doesn't like Mark but he doesn't get a vote."

"Your brother wants to protect his big sis."

Michelle gasped ignoring my comment before speaking. "Mark trains at a horse farm."

"Do you ride?"

"Sometimes." Her voice was dreamy, the Shelley-Belley I loved most.

"It must be peaceful."

"Yes, you have to come visit soon."

"I visited my sister that one weekend at her college. She watched me like a hawk."

"We'd have fun together."

"Dad says I have to be a teacher or a nurse."

"That's bull. It's almost the nineties. Women are becoming whatever they want."

"Dad's paying the bill."

"You'll do whatever you want after you finish."

"Will you visit our house this summer?"

"I'll try."

"You better."

"I'm sorry about your dad's drinking. My mom told him to quit."

"Your mom said that?"

"Yep. She told him that he needed to dump the alcohol down the drain."

I sighed and rolled over face down. "I wish he would."

Michelle paused. "My mom says it's wrong of your dad to keep drinking."

"No one can tell him not to." I propped up on my elbows, the phone hot against my ear.

"I know."

"Thanks for listening."

"I'd do anything for you."

"You didn't have to say that."

"Soon you'll be going to college. You'll have the time of your life."

"It feels far away."

"It'll come quickly."

I sat back deep into the pillows on my bed. "Does Mark drink?"

"No."

"That's a relief."

"I'm always here for you."

"Thanks. Anything wrong with Mark?"

"He works long hours. He says he's building our future."

"Will you marry him?"

"Hell no. There's no way I'm getting married."

I smiled. "Elizabeth makes me look bad. She wants to have kids but not right away."

"Having a family isn't everything, not for every woman."

"I'm glad you're my cousin."

"Me, too, Evie."

"I wish I was in your family."

"You are. My parents make me crazy, too. It wasn't easy when Dad was sneaking off with that other woman. Mom told him she wished she'd never had kids so she could leave him."

"I remember you telling me that."

"Yeah." Michelle's voice was soft.

"Your mom didn't mean it though. She was angry; she forgave him."

"Mom wasn't going to take that shit."

"I wish my mom were like that."

"She is in her own way. You don't see it being her kid. Her teaching while raising you and Elizabeth stands up to your dad."

"I guess." My voice was muffled almost all the way into the pillow.

"What?"

"Nothing. You always know when to call, Shelley."

"We'll forever be kindred sister spirits."

~8~

The snow came down hard on my way north on Route 15 from Susquehanna University, the start of my sales visits for the week. The cars were creeping. My muscles ached from gripping the steering wheel. I was in the middle of a blizzard. I had learned to prepare the car with a shovel, sleeping bag, hand and foot warmers, and plenty of food and water. It was almost my exit before settling in for the night. After checking into my hotel and waiting for the elevator, a waft of patchouli hit me like poison from the man standing by the elevator.

I was nauseous and grabbed onto the wall. Vomit came up in my mouth. I swallowed hard, backed away and searched for the restroom. Despite difficulty dragging my luggage into the bathroom, my hands landed hard on the sink and I saw the same fear I had all those years ago. I took deep breaths. The bile came up; I rushed to the toilet barely making it. The hot sour liquid surged through me. My throat burned. I hated that scent, that disgusting Patchouli, that horrible Bill from college wore. I flushed the toilet and stood with my palms flat on the sink. My splotched, tear-stained face looked back at me.

The memories came back in torrents. Wind howled outside.

Bill stood above me in his college apartment where he said he had taken me to study for exams. I was lying on the mattress on the floor that he'd pushed me onto, my underwear torn off.

"Stop teasing me." He grabbed my hands to the hard lump in his jeans. I wriggled out of his grasp.

"Take me back to my dorm right now."

"Relax," His voice rose. He pushed one hand hard on my leg pinning me down.

"You're hurting me. Stop!"

He ignored me and put his other hand under my shirt.

I tried to push him away. "I said no. Please don't do this." My voice shook and I was angry at my weakness.

He laughed. "You led me on with your beauty. Now you're going to put out."

He pushed me; I was on my back. He forced me to lie still. He climbed on top of me, his long and broad frame overpowering me. I tried to push him away.

"Don't move." His other hand was above my long sleeved top and he forcefully moved my bra away and bit my nipples.

With all the strength I had, I tried to get up. "Stop. Please don't do this."

His dick was hard and erect; he moved so it lay above my face. "You know you want it."

He let go one of my hands.

I tried to squirm away.

His fingers dug into my arms. He moved my hand to his penis.

I tried to withdraw my hand but he grabbed my forearm. "You're hurting me. Stop. Don't do this."

He moved his dick away and met my eyes with his. "Do what I say or you'll be hurting more."

"No. Please. Stop." I shouted trying to move away.

He grabbed my hand and forced me to enclose his dick, rubbing his hand over mine in fast movements.

He moaned. Then he pushed away my hand and hovered his dick by my mouth as he breathed harder.

I pursed my lips, shaking my head. He slapped my face.

"Suck my dick."

Tears fell from my face.

He pushed my mouth into it. I gagged and tried to move away. He thrust himself inside me, groaning. He went faster.

I choked and gagged. "Stop. I can't breathe." I knew he couldn't hear my blocked words.

He groaned, his breath long and filled with lust. His crushing body moved up away from me; he forced my hand on his dick with his hand over mine rubbing fast and hard.

I turned my head to the side of the bed.

"You're not finished, bitch." He took his hand away. My hand dropped.

"Stay still. Or I'll hit you again." He smiled, his face red, and his eyes wide.

I shook my head, my face wet with his sweat and my fear.

He thrust his dick between my legs. I screamed. It felt like it was ripping inside me. I tried to roll away. His sloppy wet mouth was all over my face. I cried as he panted. I couldn't move or speak.

As he pushed harder and faster, he yelled, "What a fucking beautiful cunt." Hot liquid slid down my leg.

A loud squeak startled me; I jumped. My tear-stained face stared back at me in the hotel bathroom mirror. Looking down hiding my face, I turned on the water, splashing away tears, eliminating any evidence. The door near where I stood opened all the way; I covered my face with one of the cloth towels folded neatly on the sink. Footsteps shuffled on the tile floor of the woman who walked in a bathroom stall behind me. I breathed out and took in a deep breath staring at my red eyes in the mirror. I looked down, tossed the washcloth.

I avoided eyes with anyone near me as I waited for the elevator, went to my room and cried as I unpacked and finished entering my sales calls for the day.

-9-

It was a Saturday morning in the first house I'd owned for three years. My feet stretched out on the ottoman. I turned page after page of Patrick Taylor's newest book. I savored the silence of a morning without deadlines and responsibilities.

After an hour I stood up, put the book on the end table and walked into the kitchen to make oatmeal. I walked toward the stove and filled the tea kettle. Except for the hiss of the gas stove, the house was quiet. I unhooked the phone line to avoid any distractions as I sometimes did on the weekend.

Thinking I would make a call in a few minutes, I plugged the phone line back in. The laundry in the basement beeped and I went downstairs to move the load into the dryer, another into the washer. From downstairs, I heard the phone ring and the answering machine came on. I didn't hear the message as I sorted my remaining laundry.

When I came up the stairs, I pushed play seeing my mother's caller ID on the line.

"Eve, please call right away. I've been calling all day. I'm worried about you. Maybe you've fallen down the basement steps. Eve, if you don't call, I'm driving there to make sure you're okay. Maybe you can't even reach the phone. It's bad enough you didn't call when you returned from your business trip yesterday. I had to call your sister who said she hadn't heard from you. There weren't any plane crashes on the news but maybe you were in a car accident or worse. Call me as soon as you get this." Her voice rose.

I frowned and dialed her number. The phone rang. The answering machine picked up.

"Mom, you have to stop worrying. I'm thirty years old. I'm fine. You don't need to come."

I plopped down on the couch and picked up a *Bon Appetit* magazine hoping my mom decided to work in her garden to relax instead. Twenty minutes passed. My doorbell rang multiple times. The porch door slammed. A knock pounded on the front door.

"Eve!" She shouted through the door. "You've got to open the door or I'm calling the police!"

I tossed my magazine aside on the end table and put my coffee mug on top of it, spilling the contents. I walked to the front of the house and opened the door.

"Thank god, you're safe. Why didn't you answer your phone?!"

I let her stand in the doorway. Her trench coat was buttoned unevenly. She wore a yellow and black Pirates baseball cap.

"Mom, I just came home. I don't want to be around anyone after being around people all week."

"I called you all day. You could have taken one minute to return my call; I'm not just anyone; I'm your mother." She leaned with her hand on the door frame.

I stood there, not budging. "Calm down. I don't know why you jump to these conclusions."

"You could have been sprawled on the basement floor!"

I put my hands on my hips. "This is ridiculous."

"Aren't you going to let me in?"

I sighed and moved over. "Fine."

"What were you doing?"

"I don't want you stopping at my house anytime you want."

She walked past me into my kitchen. "You sound like your father. I shouldn't have to wait to be invited. What kind of daughter says such things?! I want something to drink."

"I don't have any diet pop; I don't drink that stuff."

"Those health stores you go to are nothing but a bunch of baloney." She opened the refrigerator. "Your shelves are empty."

"I just got home; I haven't bought groceries yet. Calling seventeen times and assuming I'm sprawled at the bottom of the steps is not normal."

Mom closed the fridge and turned to me, her face softening. She reached for my hands. "Honey, I was worried; you're a young lady."

My hands hung loosely at my sides as I stepped away. "Stop worrying about me. I'm fine." My voice was even.

"After a week on the road, I need time alone."

"But, Evie, I'm your mother."

"Promise me you won't call like that again. You're acting crazy."

She got that tone in her voice. "Mothers worry. You didn't call last night when your flight landed. When I called your sister, the ringing phone woke up the kids. See what you caused?"

"I didn't cause anything." I folded my arms.

"All you had to do was pick up the phone and tell me you were okay." She searched my face.

"Mom, I was tired." My voice was thick with anger.

"You know how I worry about my girls."

"Elizabeth and I are adults. This obsessive calling has to stop."

"Eve, how can you say such a thing?"

"I told you this wasn't a good time. You need to leave." I moved toward the front door.

She followed. "But honey, I want to hear about your trip."

I opened the entry door and stood on the porch. "There's nothing to talk about. It's work. Do you really think that I can't take care of myself?"

"You're too young to understand. Wait until you have your own children."

"I'm not having kids. I told you that about a million times."

"Of course you are. You haven't found the right man."

I opened the door to the porch. "Please leave."

"Eve, don't talk to me like that." She moved her purse further up on her shoulder.

"You don't get to invade my privacy."

"It's not like I read your diary."

"Just go." My voice was loud.

She walked out.

The porch door opened and closed.

I went inside my house and moved the bolt locking the door. The laundry beep interrupted my thoughts. My bare feet padded through the kitchen, down the basement steps, and onto the cold cement floor.

— 10 —

"Hello?"

"Michelle. It's me."

"Eve. Are you driving?"

"Yeah, heading to a customer meeting in Toledo."

My fingers stretched out on the black leather steering wheel.

"Sorry about Mark. You really had horse shit delivered?"

"Yeah, I was so pissed catching them half naked in the barn. All those long hours, dinners missed because of "work." You should've seen the look on her face when she opened the door a couple days later to a hundred pounds of it on her front steps. I hid in the bushes to watch."

"What did Mark do when he saw you in the barn?"

"He looked up and pushed her away, saying he could explain. I stared at him a long time. I couldn't speak. I peeled out of the driveway."

"You should've called me."

"I dumped his stuff out on the curb. It was garbage night. Then I called a locksmith."

"Someone could've caught you doing that with the horse shit."

"He had it coming."

"Holy Shit." I answered. My belly ached from the laughter.

Joy returned to Michelle's voice. "Thanks for making me smile."

"It'll get better, Shel."

"Yeah." She paused. "I'm going to be certified in teaching."

"Wow. In Boston? What grade?"

"Middle school."

"Brave. Those are tough years."

"I need to make a difference."

"Yeah. All those kids with crazy hormones."

Michelle laughed.

"It's just like you, Shel, to keep going."

"I need a fresh beginning."

"When does the program start?"

"In a couple weeks."

"That's great."

"How're your parents?"

I clenched the steering wheel. "They have their separate lives. The same ol'."

"Sorry."

I shrugged. "It's how it is."

"Yeah." Her voice was quiet.

My throat tightened. "I'm glad you're my cuz'."

"Same here." Michelle's voice softened.

I took a deep breath and loosened my fingers. The flat highway ahead of me looked endless.

We were both quiet before she spoke again. "How's that new guy?"

"Sure you want to talk about this? I mean, with Mark?"

"I asked you, remember?"

"Alright. Darren's his name."

"Where's he from?"

"Germany."

"Cool."

"It's only been a few months. My dad likes him."

"Your mom?"

"She wants to be a grandmother again, — so I get those comments."

"Ugh."

"I know."

"Do you like him?"

"So far."

"That's good."

"Anything else new?"

"I started doing this heated yoga."

"What's it like?"

"It's 100 degrees in the room. We do all these stretching poses, one leading into another like downward dog into low push-up. It feels good in child's pose. At first I hated the practices. Now I go a couple times a week."

I passed a blue sign for a rest stop.

"I've heard it's healthy."

"Yeah. They do short meditations. You should try it. The instructors talk about letting go. Maybe it'll help with Mark."

"Maybe. I'll be alright." Her voice was quiet.

"Yoga is the closest thing I can give you, minus a hug over the phone."

"Thanks, Eve. Hug right back at ya. Even death won't separate us."

"Don't say that shit; I'm driving."

Michelle laughed.

"Don't tempt fate."

"You're being superstitious."

"I'm serious." I toggled the turn signal to turn off the highway.

~11~

After getting out of the elevator, I walked to Michelle's apartment in Virginia where she'd moved after completing her degree. It was early spring. I put down my luggage at her front door.

"Come on in, Evie." She hugged me.

A kitchen was off to the left. The apartment opened into a sitting area with two doors on either side.

"Wow. It's big. I like it."

"Thanks."

"How's teaching?"

"We're getting ready for a play later this spring."

"I bet your students love you."

Michelle smiled. "Put your stuff in there." She pointed to the left and I dropped my suitcase. I walked to stand by the counter while she cleaned up the dishes.

"How's Darren?"

I wrinkled my nose. "History."

"Sorry to hear it. What happened?"

"Workaholic."

"You deserve more."

I shrugged.

She turned off the water, leaned across the sink and put her hand on my arm.

I looked up at her.

"There's someone better out there and he's waiting for you."

"Being alone makes me feel bad. All my friends are married."

"Do what you love and be happy. Forget what everyone else thinks."

"Let's talk about something else."

Her voice softened. "I want the best for you."

"Let's change the subject, okay?" I looked at her eyes.

"I know you're hurting. It's hard being alone at first. You're braver than you think. You're better off without him."

I turned to face her. "I want to believe it. I'm trying." My face burned hot and I swallowed hard.

"You can. Look, I have some surprises this weekend. First, I'm taking you to the Italian restaurant."

I attempted a weak smile. "Am I buying?"

Crows' feet spread around Michelle's eyes. "I'm afraid so. But the laughs are free." She reached out to hug me. "I'm proud of you; you know that, right?"

After dinner, Michelle made a cocktail back at the apartment.

"You okay having one?"

"Sure. Wine is off limits; that's Dad's problem. Cocktails are approved." I put my thumb up.

The ice clinked in the glasses as Michelle made the piña coladas.

I stared at the mostly blank watercolor with one or two light colored washes on the easel.

"Are you painting?" She called from the kitchen.

I smiled and turned back. "I was just thinking that about you with that canvas over there. I'm working on an oil painting now, a water scene. What's that going to be?" I pointed.

"A horse farm where I've been riding when I can scrape together enough cash. It's Moksha Equestrian Farms. I needed that place. Moksha is a Hindu and Buddhist term about letting go and releasing: the ultimate liberation."

"Wow. I can't wait to see it finished."

"Yeah. School keeps me busy. There's not much time for anything else. Cheers!" She raised her glass and gave me the other.

"To my favorite cousin!" I clinked her glass.

After talking a while, I switched over to water. "Time for bed." I stood up and stretched.

"I have more surprises coming; just wait."

I smiled. "I've missed you, Shel."

The next morning while Michelle cleaned up the dishes, I wandered into her living room and started thumbing through her sketchbook.

"You've been drawing?" My fingers skimmed the pages as I saw small portraits, a bunch on one page. "This one's handsome!"

"Don't look at that. It's nothing." Michelle rushed over to where I was standing, snatching the sketchbook away.

"Why? Michelle, what's wrong?"

"That's just old stuff. That was Mark. I was just looking back at old pictures."

My eyes searched hers. "Are you sure that's all it is?"

She shook her head. "I forgot it was out. I didn't want you to see it."

I reached for it to study the drawing.

Michelle put her hand down on it before I did. "Look, it doesn't matter. I forgot to put it away before you came."

"Why were you looking at it? It's been over a year since you left Boston. Why would you waste time looking back?"

"I'm human. I was looking at old sketches. It means nothing."

"If you say so."

Michelle wouldn't meet my eyes and walked back to the kitchen to finish cleaning up.

"Is there anything you want to tell me?"

"Did you sleep enough? You're being aggressive."

"No. I'm trying to understand why you're acting weird." I walked to the counter pulling out the stool to face her. "Will you just look at me?"

Michelle looked down holding the sponge wiping

down imaginary crumbs. "I wasn't going to tell you, but you started looking at those pictures. I can't lie to you."

"You better not say he's the one and similar shit."

"Eva, don't say it like that."

I shook my head, raised my eyebrows. "My god, Michelle, what are you doing? Do you not remember what he did to you with that woman — all those lies. How do you know he's not lying to you again? You'll never know. I can't believe you're doing this. When did it start? How long has it been?" I ignored the shadow crossing her face.

She turned away grabbing her jacket and purse. "I'm not talking to you about this now. This was supposed to be our time." She reached across the sink and put her hand on my arm. "Let's enjoy our time together, please."

Her eyes penetrated mine.

I swallowed hard. "You promise we'll talk about this."

"Yes."

I watched her face relax. I didn't push and remained silent.

"Look, there's a new portrait gallery you're going to love. Are you ready to go?"

"Yes." I avoided her face. I took a deep breath, grabbing my coat and bag. We walked to the car talking about nothing.

We wandered around the gift shop and then into the gallery after buying tickets. Michelle read each sign by each painting. I moved quickly from one to another. I didn't see her after a while, sat on one of the benches, and waited.

When she found me, she sat down. "I thought you'd be happy here. We always share our love of art together."

I looked straight ahead, my voice quiet. "It is nice. It was kind of you to take me here."

"Look at me."

My voice was low over the hum of museum visitors as I kept staring ahead. "I can't stop thinking about what you said yesterday, about being brave and being on my own. Mark hurt you in the worst way. How can you be with him after all that?"

She shifted to face me. "I told you I didn't want to talk about this now."

We sat in silence.

Shel slid her arm through mine.

I sighed and dared a glimpse at her. "Just tell me."

"Not now."

"Why?"

"Listen to me. This weekend was for you and me. I wanted to tell you later, just until I knew for sure."

"What aren't you telling me? You better not be marrying him. That's like going to jail; look at my parents."

Michelle pulled her arm away and put her hands on the ledge of the seat pushing herself back. "We're moving in together and planning our wedding. He moved down here to be with me six months ago." Her voice was quiet and even.

I stood up to walk away. Instead I turned to her, one hand on my hip. "How could you do this? After everything you've taught me about being independent?"

The docents looked over at us, our voices loud over the bustling of the crowd.

Michelle stood to face me.

My lips were tight. "I don't even know what I'm doing here. You told me about being brave but you're going back to him! I looked up to you. I believed in you. Look at what he did to you."

Michelle tried to reach out but I stepped back.

"Everything you ever taught me about being strong is a lie. Mark will do something awful again. He doesn't respect you." My voice was louder than I meant and my face felt hot. I breathed in and out to keep from crying.

"Mark is sorry. He isn't like that. Eva, he's the one. I forgave him. I didn't want to tell you like this."

"Like what?" My words were pointed.

"Being with Darren hurt you. I know how vulnerable you feel. I remember."

"I don't need your pity. Get away from me." I stood.

I saw Michelle's hurt and I hated being the cause of it. But I couldn't move.

People in the hall turned, watching.

Her voice was soft. "I wanted to help you feel better with this weekend."

My throat was tight. I couldn't speak.

People moved around us in the crowded gallery, the hum of talking as if we weren't there.

"You're not helping me. Mark is going to shit all over you again. You said you wouldn't marry because not every woman needs that. I thought you were strong. You were my one role model. I bet this stupid surprise was to ride horses. And I'd be paying of course."

Michelle looked at me a long time. "I know this hurts and you probably don't mean these things. I'm leaving to go home with or without you." She turned and walked away. I watched her and then ran, catching up.

"Wait, Michelle! I'm sorry." I called after her.

Running, I followed her.

The ride home was silent.

She pulled into her parking space. "You need to leave."

At her apartment, I packed my things. She walked me to my car.

"Let's start fresh."

"No."

"Michelle!"

She shook her head. "I have papers to grade."

"What about the surprise? We'll start again. We can do this. Let's figure this out. I'll be calm. I'll listen. I swear."

"It's too late. And, yes, you got it right. It was riding horses, at that place of that watercolor I'm doing. I was going to take you to Moksha, I thought you'd find the peace there that I found. I saved for a while. It was going to be my treat."

I reached to hug her to apologize, but she backed away. Heaviness filled my stomach. I stood in front of her as my tears fell.

She blinked many times.

"I'm sorry for earlier. Yes, I'm upset. I'm afraid I'll never find anyone who accepts me." My throat thickened.

"You need to go." She crossed her arms.

"Why can't we start over?"

Instead of answering me, she moved her fingers across her right eye and wiped the side of her temple.

"I'll come down next month."

She rubbed the same eye. "I'm leading the school play; it'll consume all my free time."

"We can find time; we always do."

She blinked.

We stood apart from each other and I left.

~12~

Two months passed after my visit to Michelle's. The phone rang.

"Aunt Patsy. It's good to hear your voice."

"Eva, how are you?"

"I'm good. How's Michelle?"

She paused. "Did I catch you at a good time?"

"I had to run for the phone. I was upstairs. What's going on?"

"You better sit down."

"Why? What's wrong?"

"Michelle's in the hospital. She's being treated for cancer."

"Wait. What?" I grasped for the counter in front of me and squeezed my hand into a tight fist. My nails dug into my palms.

"Michelle has stomach cancer. Her survival rate is not good. She's getting more tests."

I held my breath. Tears came down my face as I stared out the window seeing nothing. I couldn't speak. I took deep breaths, trying not to betray my shaking voice. "Do my parents know?"

"I'm calling them next. I wanted to tell you first."

I was trying to breathe, trying to shake away the words.

"Evie, are you still there?"

"Yes," I whispered. I swallowed hard. "She is young; she'll be okay. She can fight this. She's healthy. I just saw her." My voice broke.

"We don't know that."

I breathed out. "What is the survival rate?"

"It's very low. She didn't go to the doctor when she should've. She never took care of herself. The growth shows she's had the cancer a few months."

"What? A few months?"

Guilt surged through me how we parted ways.

I could hear Aunt Patsy's breathing.

"Where is she?"

"George Washington Cancer Care Hospital."

"Why is this happening? She's young."

"Evie, we don't know. I'm sorry to tell you all this."

"Hmm." My voice was soft. I tried to breathe, my throat tightening. "How long has she been in the hospital?"

"A couple days."

My heart was racing. I was sweating.

"I love you."

I answered her, not remembering the details of writing down the hospital room number, the phone number, clicking the phone to hang up, and leaving it on the floor as it made the loud sound after the disconnect.

I fell to the floor and cradled myself in a tight ball. I cried. I spoke aloud, "No. Not Michelle. No," I sat on the kitchen floor like that for hours. "This isn't right. This is a lie," I whispered. This is going to be a horrible dream when I wake up. I'm going to call her tomorrow, apologize how we left things. That's all this is. It's a sign to break our silence. None of this is real.

Eventually I went to bed, not remembering getting up or sleeping.

The next day I dialed the number for Michelle's room. The nurse patched me through.

"Hello?" Michelle's voice was quiet.

"It's me. I wanted to call last night but your mom said you were sleeping." I gripped the phone.

"It's okay. My brother just left."

"I'm glad Rory was there. How are you?" My face felt hot.

"I don't know. I'm not sure, shocked."

I heard sadness in her voice.

"I want this to be a lie. I told myself that after your mom called."

"I knew you would call."

"I pushed you too much at the gallery. I'm sorry. Your mom said it's been a few months. Why didn't you just tell me you were tired then? I knew I wouldn't say anything right." Sweat gripped me; my voice broke.

"I don't care about that. You called me now."

I didn't answer. It was my fault. I made her worse.

"How did you get there? How did you learn —?" I couldn't say the word.

"My mom didn't tell you?"

"I don't remember everything she said. I don't know why, maybe shock."

"I was admitted two days ago. I drove myself to the emergency room. Something didn't feel right. They found the cancer. They've been doing tests since then."

"What are they testing?"

"To see how far it's spread, if it's treatable."

"Oh." My voice was high. I swallowed hard as I waited for silent tears to fall. I breathed out, my mouth away from the phone. "I'll come see you. I don't know how to help you: I can't help you. But I can be there." My voice broke and I let her hear me cry.

Her voice was jagged. "Rory dropped off some things."

"I can come."

"No. You can't see me like this."

"Why? I don't care how you look. I want to hold your hand; I love you."

"Not right now." Her voice was almost a whisper.

"I want to help."

"You're already doing it."

The hum of the phone line filled the space between us.

"Stomach cancer. They're sure?" I said it, the ugly words out of my mouth.

"Yes," she whispered.

"You're young and strong though. That has to help."

Neither of us spoke.

"My thirty-eighth birthday's coming up. September 11th." Her voice was soft.

"Don't worry; we'll celebrate." I tried to be upbeat.

"Thanks."

"You're going to beat this." My hand ached holding the phone; a knuckle cracked.

Her voice was quiet. "Remember when we last saw each other?"

"I never forgot it. I felt terrible. I still do. I wish I'd stayed. I should have made you let me."

"I regretted making you leave."

"We've always talked everything through. I hated not being in touch." I wiped away a tear.

"I wanted you to ride the horses with me that weekend."

"We still can. We will."

She didn't answer.

"Everything will turn out alright. We're Armstrongs, strong as an ox." I thumped my chest.

"Yeah," she whispered.

"Maybe there are some handsome male nurses."

"Hmm."

"I'm saying everything wrong. I can't believe this."

"Neither can I."

"At least you have your clothes now. You're not flapping in the breeze anymore. I know how those hospital gowns are."

"What do you think is flapping in the breeze?" Humor hung in her voice.

"Whatever might flap. Flap-flap!"

Her laugh was soft.

"You get two ties in the back to keep yourself covered. I remember what that was like when I'd been in the hospital."

"You're ridiculous." Laughter returned to her tired voice.

"The answer my friend is flappin' in the breeze ..." I sung to her.

She sang the words with her beautiful choir voice.

I laughed hard; tears came out of my eyes. My belly ached. "Flappin' in the breeze," I half sung.

"—Eeze." She sang on key.

"Mi-chelle, ma belle," I sang louder.

"Ha ha, very funny."

"You know it, Shelley-Belley."

"Don't call me that, Evie!" I heard her smile. "And, Cuz, you're a horrible singer."

"Enthusiasm doesn't count?! I'm a great singer!"

"Greatly off-key."

"I wish I was there with you now." My throat tightened.

"It's like you're already here."

After over an hour of talking about nothing, my ear cramped.

"I don't want to hang up. But I should let you rest."

"I am tired."

"When will your parents arrive?"

"In a few days. They're driving from Florida."

"Seems like they would make an exception and fly just this once."

"I told my mother that but she is convinced the plane will crash."

I breathed out.

"I won't know anything for sure until they run more tests."

"It'll be okay. I better let you rest."

"Thanks for calling and making me laugh. You make me happy when no one else can."

"Will Rory come tomorrow?"

"Yes. He'll be with me. I'll never be alone. Someone is often here checking on me."

Neither of us said anything. Only the humming phone line filled the silence for a full minute.

"What about Mark?"

"What?"

"Is he there? You never mentioned him."

"He changed his mind about us. I don't know where he is. It doesn't matter."

"Oh my god." Shame washed over me. "I'm so sorry. I said terrible things. You were trying to be kind and I — "

"Don't think about that anymore. None of that matters."

"I could pummel him."

"You can't be like that. You sound like Rory."

"Oh, Michelle." I tightened my face, cradled the phone in my ear and covered my eyes.

"This isn't fair."

She didn't answer. "I need to rest."

"I wish I'd ridden horses with you that day." I blurted out.

"You'll always be with me, Evie. Bye." The phone didn't click.

My words were fast and desperate. "Shelley, it's 'see you later.' We never say good-bye. And then your line is 'after a while crocodile.'"

"I know, kiddo. I'm falling asleep."

I made my voice strong. "See you later." I hung up the phone after she clicked first. I stared at it while my mind ran wild.

Each day that week I tried to call Michelle but there was no answer. I even tried calling her cell phone, but it rang once and went dead every time. After the end of the week, her mother answered the hospital phone.

"Aunt Patsy, how are you? How's Michelle? May I talk to her?"

"The doctor's here. I can't talk right now."

"I can wait."

"It's going to be a long time."

"When should I call back?"

"Not today. Everyone's worn out."

"How's Michelle? I've been trying to call."

"Eva, I can't talk. Bye." She hung up the phone.

I called again later in the day.

"Uncle Jack. How are you?"

His voice was quiet. "Everyone's fine here, Evie."

"I need to talk to Michelle."

"She can't talk."

"Why? What's happening? I want to help."

"We have everything we need here. Michelle sleeps a lot."

"When is a good time?"

"It's better that you wait. She's very sick."

"Uncle Jack, Shelley's practically my sister. I have to do something."

"We'll call if we need anything. The doctor is here now. Take care, Evie."

"But Uncle Jack —"

The phone line went dead and I held it in my hand. My heart was racing as I sat on the kitchen floor and put my head in my hands.

Two days later, I reached Aunt Patsy and Uncle Jack staying at Michelle's apartment.

"Hi, honey."

"Aunt Patsy. My family and I want to see Michelle. I packed the car to drive down first thing tomorrow. I'll be there by mid-morning." I blurted out the words.

"We have everyone we need here. Please don't come."

"But I have to see her. She needs me."

"She's tired. Visitors wear her out."

"But I'm not a visitor. I'm her favorite cousin. It's not a far drive and Elizabeth wants to see her, too. We want to give her our support."

"Michelle has everyone she needs."

I heard Uncle Jack in the background.

"Michelle asked that you and your family to not come. She's afraid you'll remember her like this. You wouldn't recognize her."

"I need to see her."

Uncle Jack got on the line. "Eva, I know this is hard. It's difficult for everyone, but stop pushing your Aunt Patsy. This is our daughter. She is weak and frail. I know you love her. The doctor said even if she shows signs of improvement, she's susceptible to viruses. You travel a lot. Today the doctor has asked that visitors stay away."

I sighed. "Uncle Jack, I'm not sick; I could wear a mask and gloves. I just want to hold her hand. Please put Aunt Patsy back on."

I heard the sound of the phone being put down.

"Hello, honey. There's a new experimental drug. If she responds well to it, we'll bring her home. Her hair is starting to grow back. We're going to put her on a medical flight to Florida. When she gets better, you can see her in the spring. She can teach where we live."

"What?"

"It'll be better for her if we can care for her from our home."

"Is traveling good for her?"

"Evie, we've already decided. We're doing what's best."

"I need to see her. Don't you understand what she means to me?" My voice broke.

"Keep sending those letters. We hang them all around her room. She smiles at your funny stories. Don't give up hope. Say a prayer. You'll see her again."

"But, Aunt Patsy—"

"Honey, it's been a long day. I'm tired and Uncle Jack is calling me. Keep writing letters. It makes her smile."

"I need to see her."

"You will, later in the spring when she's feeling better. Have faith."

That night many dreams came with no memories of them in the morning.

I picked up the phone to dial.

"Mom," I mumbled.

"Good morning, Eva. Oh dear, you don't sound awake. Are you sick?"

"I just woke up. Last night I talked to Aunt Patsy. She says they have everyone they need. She said Michelle didn't want me — us — to remember her like that. And now the doctor says if she catches a virus, it could kill her. She made her family promise to not let us see her. But she's alive now. I don't want to wait until spring."

"We have to respect her and her family's wishes."

"I need to see her."

"She wants you to remember her as full of life. And we have to listen to the doctor."

"I need her to know how much I care."

"She already knows." Her voice was firm.

"Whenever I call, she never answers."

"If her parents have decided they don't want us there, we can't do anything about it. Try praying."

"Religion and prayers are a waste of time."

"Eva! I know you're upset, but don't say such things."

"I called you for help, Mom." My throat choked with tears.

"You have to listen to what the doctor said."

"Michelle is trying to be brave. But she needs me."

"Start praying."

I gasped and hung up.

The next day I met Gwen at the coffee shop. We'd been friends about ten years, though I was starting to lose count. She knew my father from hiking trips he had led. Dad was like her Pittsburgh Dad, since she was far from her own in Wisconsin.

She put her long dark wavy hair back in a pony tail and short wisps fell out.

"You look like a model that just stepped out of REI," I mused.

Gwen smiled. "Yeah. They were having sales. I needed an outfit to go with my Mary Janes." She lifted her foot.

I looked under the table and gave a weak smile. "Nice."

"How's your cousin?" She took a sip of her latté.

"Not good. I need to be there."

Gwen softened her voice. "The timing isn't right."

"That's bullshit and you know it."

Gwen's eyes widened.

"Sorry. I didn't mean — I can't do a damned thing for her. I'm sitting here having coffee while she's in that hospital bed. I'm the one that makes her laugh. She told me that."

"But you can't go there."

"Oh, the hell, I can't." I stood up.

"This is crazy. They don't want you there."

I looked down at it. "Right." I took a sip of my mocha. Some of it spilled on the table. "I'll get a to-go cup. I'm driving down there now."

"You can't go now. It's 8:00 at night. You're an early morning person. It'll take you five hours. Where will you stay?"

"I don't care."

"Eva, sit down and think about this for a minute. The doctor said she could easily catch a virus or infection. You need to stay here."

I remained standing and looked down at Gwen.

"I know this is hard. Please sit."

I pulled the chair out and sat down hard. My hands wiped away the tears. "Sorry."

"It isn't easy, I know. Have you gone to yoga lately?"

"Yoga?! I'm doing nothing for her."

"Yoga relaxes you. If she recovers, you'll see her in the spring. She wants you to remember good times if —."

I looked up at her and dried a tear with the back of my hand. "The last time we saw each other was at that gallery. We argued. It was my fault. I need to see her forgiveness. And yoga isn't going to change anything; she'll still have cancer."

"She does forgive you, she told you that on the phone about wishing she'd asked you to stay. Eva, take care of yourself."

"How do you know she forgives me?"

"I know because of how you talk about her."

"I want to see her, to tell her how much she means to me."

"I watched my aunt die. I know what it looks like. It's hard. I'm not saying you can't handle it. I'm saying it's hard to forget those memories. Your cousin wants you to remember the fun. She's telling you it's okay. You two are connected; you don't even have to be in the same room."

"Maybe." My shoulders fell.

"Promise me you won't go. You have to listen to the doctors. Go to yoga. It'll help."

"I'll try." My throat was tight.

"Think about it."

"I can't talk about this anymore."

"You're doing everything you can. I'm sure she feels it."

"Let's move onto some other topic."

Gwen leaned back in her chair and took a drink from her mug.

I drove home after I met Gwen.

I picked up the phone to call Michelle. The phone rang and rang. No one picked up. I called the hospital again, the main line asking for the nurse.

"Hello?" I'm trying to reach Michelle Armstrong. Her room number is 1609."

"I'll connect you."

"Wait. I just tried. Why did no one answer?"

"The doctor could be in there. Maybe she's sleeping. Are you family?"

"Yes."

"I'll try ringing the line again."

"Thank you."

"Sorry. No answer."

"Could you check on her?"

"I'm the only nurse here now. I can't leave my station."

"Why won't anyone help me? I need to be sure Michelle is okay."

"Calm down."

My pacing was making me dizzy. I opened the refrigerator, saw nothing and slammed it shut.

"My cousin is dying and you won't even check on her."

"You're hurting my ears. Stop yelling."

"I need to know how she is."

"I can't help you."

The line went dead in my hand. I walked to the kitchen cabinet and smashed plate after plate against the wall hearing each one crash, the glass shards going everywhere. I sobbed and threw another harder at the wall.

It was quiet a while.

I got up to sweep up the glass and went to get the vacuum cleaner. I put on Beethoven's "Moonlight Sonata" and walked to the couch and cried into a pillow until I fell asleep.

The next morning sunlight filled the living room. I thought about what Gwen said and went to yoga, dedicating my class to Michelle. After showering, I sat down and wrote a letter on a blank notecard with a silhouetted horse in an orange sunset.

Dear Michelle,

I've tried to see you, but your parents tell me you don't want us there. They also said about the doctor not allowing visitors because of possible infections. They said you are the one asking us to stay away.

We think of you everyday. Mom prays; Elizabeth and her family do, too. Dad wants to see you better, but he doesn't talk about it. He's been drinking a lot, more than usual, according to Mom. You're the only one I could ever tell that to.

During my yoga classes the instructor says to think about someone who needs love, strength or good health wishes and dedicate the practice to that person. I think about you every time.

I'm proud of you.

You and I were supposed to grow old together laughing about our great times, but I shouldn't think about that now; I always thought we would.

If it's too hard to live, let go. I don't want you to leave, but if you're suffering, don't hold on. I don't want to say good-bye. I can't. See you later, okay?

Love you forever.
Evie

Two days later, the connection of holding on for Michelle felt broken. I couldn't pick up the pen and write her. I thought, *she's gone* and picked up the phone even though it was almost 11:00. Her parents were night owls.

"Aunt Patsy, I hope it's not too late."

"We're still up."

"How's Michelle?"

"She died last night."

"Why didn't you tell me?" My face collapsed as I lay in bed with the cordless phone crushing my ear.

"We were going to tell you later on the weekend."

"I needed to know when it happened."

"We were protecting you."

"I honored your wish not to visit. I didn't like it. You kept my family from her and now this. What's wrong with you? I'll never see her again."

"That's not true. You'll see her in the spirit world."

"You all said good-bye but you took that away from me."

"It's been hard watching my daughter die."

"But you were there. I could do nothing for her."

"I had to protect you both. We've always thought of you as one of our own."

"If that was true, why did you make sure I'd never see her again?"

The line was silent.

"I let myself believe I'd see her in Florida in the spring. I let myself hope. And for what?"

"She was suffering. It was her time."

"No."

"I'm sorry. We're very tired. It's been hard."

"This can't be right."

"Michelle's gone." Aunt Patsy's voice was dreamy.

The line was quiet again until I spoke, my voice soft. "I wrote this one letter, the one with the horses on it. I told her how proud I was of her."

"Yes. She received it."

"Did she say anything?"

"She was weak. She wasn't talking much in the last few days."

The phone line hummed.

"She smiled and kept the card over her heart after we read it."

I blinked quickly, tears falling. "Why didn't you call me? You knew how much she meant to me."

"Eva, —"

"I was never there with Michelle holding her hand and telling her stories to take her mind off the — the cancer." The word fell out of my mouth like poison.

"Your letters told those stories. She loved them. She adored all the pretty pictures you took for her. You brought color and warmth to those white hospital walls. She felt the laughter in your words. You and Michelle had a special connection."

I cried, no sound from my voice. I took a breath wiping the hot tears off my face. "Were you with her when she —?" I couldn't say the word aloud.

"No. We'd left for dinner after Uncle Jack sat with her for a while."

Panic rose in my chest. "She was by herself?"

"No. The nurses were there." She paused. "Do you want to know what she did?" She didn't wait for me to speak. "She told the nurses to give her balloons and flowers to the people who didn't have any visitors. The nurses said, 'why not give the balloons to the kids?' Michelle said, 'No; they have their families.' She wanted the people dying alone to feel cared for."

I was quiet, taking it in.

"How's your job?"

"How can you ask me that when your daughter just died?"

"I've accepted her death. It was coming for a while. You need to let go your anger. It will eat at you. You're like Michelle was and Rory —"

"Aunt Patsy!"

"You should go to sleep. You have work tomorrow."

"I don't care about that! I can't believe you would even bring that up. How can I care about anything else when Michelle — the person who meant the most to me is gone?" I sobbed into the phone.

"Oh, Eva, honey. Don't be upset. Peace will come. You have to let it; that's what I've done. She was not meant to live like this. She worked hard and didn't rest enough. The chemotherapy was devastating. Be glad you didn't see what it did. I'm hanging up and going to sleep."

"Aunt Patsy, but—"

"Eva, I need to get ready for bed. It's late." My aunt's soft voice sounded like Michelle's.

I gripped the phone; I whispered, "Goodbye," the line still active.

"Remember, Michelle isn't suffering anymore."

I clicked the off button on my phone and stared straight ahead in my bedroom, and then dialed Mom's number.

She answered, disoriented and tired. "Hello?"

"Mom." I whispered between tears. "Were you sleeping?"

"No." Which meant yes. Mom frequently fell asleep on the couch around 9:00 watching mystery crime shows.

"Michelle died."

"What?"

I spoke the words loud and fast. "She's dead."

"Evie."

"You told me to have hope, faith." The words spat out of me.

"How do you know about Michelle?"

"I called Aunt Patsy. I couldn't write Michelle. It didn't feel right."

"What time is it?"

"I don't know. 11:30."

"You shouldn't have called them so late."

"They never let us see her again." My words were loud in my dark bedroom.

"Michelle didn't want us to see her like that."

"I should've gone down there."

"You had to listen to what the doctor said."

"None of that matters. She died. She would've been there for me. She needed me and I listened to you and everyone else about this faith crap. Aunt Patsy is acting like her death is no big deal. All she could say was 'she's in the spirit world now.' Like that changes anything."

"Eva! Don't say that. You don't know what it's been like for Aunt Patsy. Maybe it's a relief for her."

"A relief? Michelle is dead. That's horrible."

"Eva, I know you're upset, but when time passes, you'll understand."

"Faith, what a god-damned load of bull."

"Did you want Michelle to suffer? I know you didn't. I know her cancer tore you up inside. Eventually you'll be less sad. You'll remember the good times. Maybe in a few months, you can write her a letter and tell her everything you wanted to say."

"Mom, she's gone. She's not going to hear any more of my thoughts."

"I know she meant everything to you."

"Aunt Patsy took away my right to say good-bye."

"You're upset, Evie; sometimes it's better not to react. And you should have waited to hear from Aunt Patsy."

"Why pretend it's fine all the time?"

"Eve, I know Michelle just died. Take some deep breaths. Go downstairs and make some tea."

"I should have gone to see her!"

"She didn't want you to remember her like that."

"How can you say that?"

"You kept writing her letters. You never gave up. Many people aren't able to stay in touch; you showed great courage. You could've stopped writing her, but you gave her comfort."

"She still died, so nothing I did matters."

"Yes, she did. And what you did for her does matter."

"I don't know."

"She'll always be with you. She'll never be more than a thought away."

"But I wasn't ready."

"No one was, but it was her time."

My face was wet with tears.

"Make yourself some chamomile tea. Have some of your vanilla yogurt. Take some deep breaths. It'll get a little easier after some time. Your tears of love are the last step of saying good-bye."

A few months after Michelle's death, Mom greeted me on the phone.

"Michelle wouldn't want you to be sad." Concern weighed heavily in her voice.

"I don't remember what Michelle's hug feels like. I'll never get that back."

"Michelle is with you, no matter what you remember. Let me tell you a Thai tradition that helped me once."

I gripped the phone.

"When your dad was stationed in the Philippines, one night in Bangkok, we watched people at the edge of the sea light little boats with candles. The story was that you let the boats float to cast away your grief. Think of all your sadness and imagine letting it drift away. Michelle wouldn't want you missing her like this. You have to live your life."

I closed my eyes seeing and hearing the image, a small lighted boat on a choppy dark sea in the black of night. Sadness and anger drifted like dark liquid. I opened my eyes. Heaviness remained in the pit of my belly.

As the days, weeks and months passed by, that image of the Thai boats played over and over in my mind.

~13~

In early May, the spring following Michelle's death, I received a card in the mail from Aunt Patsy with Michelle's finished watercolor on the front, the one I'd asked her about. A brown and white embossed horse was running off into a distant field. A creek flowed in the foreground. Green-leafed trees and pines stood off to the side.

Opening the card revealed the words:

What: Michelle Armstrong Memorial
Where: Moksha Equestrian Farm, McLean, Virginia
When: Saturday, May 26th

Dear Evie,

Come say good-bye to our dear Michelle. We're letting her ashes go where she loved to ride.

Love,
Aunt Patsy & Uncle Jack

We sat under the tent, a stainless steel urn sitting on the table in front of us.

Michelle's immediate family sat in the front: Rory, Jess, Uncle Jack and Aunt Patsy. A row of Uncle Jack's siblings were behind them. Then it was Mom, Elizabeth, and me in the next row back.

Aunt Patsy stood up. She opened a prayer book to the bookmarked page and began to read about the heavens reaching down for Michelle's ravaged soul and body.

I clenched my fists, turning away. Sweat flashed above my lips. I could've read from a book of poetry but brought nothing. I looked straight ahead at nothing, trying not to blink, wishing I didn't hear the words. My fingers ached and the back of my head hurt. A dull pain ached in my chest. My stomach felt hollow and though I had eaten little, nausea grew. I couldn't stand up and do anything for Michelle, not when she had the cancer and not now.

"Do you still go to church?" I asked one day when we walked outside Michelle's apartment.

"No, I stopped."

"Same here."

"Organized religion is too much about control and politics," Michelle turned to me as she walked.

I nodded.

"I'm a Buddhist now."

"I know."

"It speaks to me like nothing else."

Michelle stopped walking. "When I die, make sure there's none of that churchy stuff in my funeral."

"Woah. Don't say stuff like that."

"You know how our family is. Promise."

"This conversation is ridiculous. We shouldn't talk about these things."

"Come on, promise me." She stopped and looked at me.

"You're crazy. You're not going anywhere." I grabbed her arm, my own hairs rising. Heat surged through my face.

"Say it." Her lips pursed together.

"Fine, I promise, as long as you stop talking like this." I tried to pick up the pace.

She reached for my arm. I turned and she caught my eyes. She spit on her hand and put it out. "Shake hands now."

"Gross. I'm not doing that."

"Do it." Her eyes drilled into mine.

After scrunching my face, I spit and we shook hands.

-14-

Six months had passed since Michelle's memorial.

My enclosed porch door slammed. Dad stood outside the window from my living room. I was working downstairs on my mosaic tile dining room table, updating contacts in my database for the latest marketing mailing. Papers and folders were spread everywhere. I stood up, stretched and walked to the door, opening it. Tall and broad-shouldered in front of me, he turned, pointing to the walnut dining room table I'd moved out onto the porch for him to pick up.

"Where are the chairs, Evie?"

"Why do you want it?"

He looked at me awhile. His lips pursed in a thin line. His eyes squinted.

I braced.

"Didn't your mother tell you?"

I looked at him and shifted my feet, moving my weight from the right to the left. My body ached as if we'd been standing a long time.

"I bought a house three weeks ago. I served your mother with divorce papers this morning."

"What?" I felt nauseous and light-headed but there was nothing to grab onto; I stared back at Dad, hoping he'd steady me. He looked away.

My gaze shifted to the wall beneath the picture of Slovenian friends I'd made in Croatia, a recent vacation.

"I'm divorcing your mother. Do you have any chairs for the table?"

My eyes shifted back to Dad's. "They're in the basement."

"Will you get them?"

I turned around, walking in my bare feet through the house and down the basement steps. Heat surged through my chest. My breaths came quicker and shorter. It was hard to swallow. Tears of panic came. Dad didn't like displays of upset emotions. I wiped the back of my hand across my face.

I returned with a chair. He took it and walked out the porch door. He went down the stoop toward my driveway where he'd parked his pickup truck.

A second chair was in my hands. While stone-faced, I walked up the stairs again.

Each time I gave him one, Dad answered, "do you have another," until he had all four.

From my front steps by the iron railing, I watched Dad load the last chair in the bed of his white truck next to the table. After he finished, he walked to the driver's side.

"Dad! Is there someone else?" I gripped the railing.

"No. I want to be alone."

His words slapped me.

"I need to know what to expect."

He was silent, standing by his truck, looking up at me. The muscles in his face loosened.

"What's your new number?"

Dad's face relaxed. "The same. I didn't have to change it from my office at your mother's."

I stared back at him.

He glanced at me and climbed into his truck, backed out of my driveway, and down the street. The kitchen furniture in the back of his truck was driven away, the white pick-up turning left up the next hill until it could no longer be seen.

The door slammed behind me. I walked up the two flights to my office carrying my laptop and folders.

My work Email stared in front of me. I read the first message three times without knowing the content.

I picked up my cell phone. "Gwen, it's me. My dad came for the kitchen table."

"What?"

"He's divorcing my mom. He needs it for his new house. He's moving there this afternoon."

"Wait. What're you talking about?"

"This is it. My parents are finished. Finally." I spat out the words.

"Did you talk to your mom?"

"No. Dad just left."

"I'm sorry, Eva. Gees. It's not going to be easy. Does your sister know?"

"I don't know. I found out five minutes ago. I called you first."

Neither of us spoke for a moment.

"Your parents weren't happy."

"How can forty-three years of them together come to an end?"

"What else did he say?"

"The table was for his new house. I didn't even know he was looking. He gave my mother divorce papers this morning."

The line was quiet.

"Are you there?"

"Yes. I was listening. It could be better for everyone."

"I should be happy, but I'm not. My parents are in their sixties. When we were younger, Elizabeth and I used to pray for this, when I believed there was a god. I gave up thinking they'd ever get divorced. I was used to Dad's drinking and Mom's silence. But now that it's here, —"

"It's hard."

"I can't believe it."

"It's understandable."

"I thought I'd be happy when this day came. What if Mom decides to move in with me?"

"There's no reason to think about that now."

"I should let you get back to your work day."

"We can talk anytime, Eva. I have time right now."

"I better go." I looked at the white screen in front of me.

"Call me whenever —"

"After years of wanting him to leave us alone, why do I feel bad?"

"You're in shock."

"Why do I feel panicked?"

"The strong emotions will fade."

After hanging up with Gwen, I looked at my phone and dialed Mom's number.

"Dad was here. He came for the table. He said he told you to tell me."

"Eve, I'm sorry how you found out. But we're not getting divorced; we'll be separated."

"What?!"

"He moved out this morning. One of his hiking friends helped him take out the furniture. He bought a house ..."

"I know, he told me. But he said he served you with divorce papers."

"I'm not getting a divorce. I'll convince him to separate."

"That's not what Dad wants. Mom, how are you? Really?" I pushed.

"I'm fine. We didn't have the same friends."

"You don't have to fake being happy. It's me."

"Eva!" Mom's voice softened.

"Look where the pretending got you?"

"How can you say that? We'll be separated. I'm not getting a divorce."

"Right." Heat rose in my chest. "Dad's not going to go for that. You know how he is." Putting my ear on the phone, I leaned my elbows on the desk, shook my head and put my hands in my face though there were no tears.

"I'm not going to be like one of those divorcées."

I sat up. "You better tell Elizabeth, because I'm not doing it."

"I'll tell her. She'll understand because she has a family."

I flattened my hands on the table, my fingers stiff and tight.

"Fine. It's not my news anyway."

"What have you been up to this week?"

"What?"

"Did you have a good weekend? Did you go biking?"

"Mom, I can't believe you. You're acting like this is no big deal!"

"It's nothing to worry about."

"How long have you known?"

"Since this morning before he came to your house. There was no time to call; I had to re-organize the house where he took the furniture to fill up the empty spaces."

"Are you really sorry?"

"We both love you. This isn't your fault."

"If you loved Elizabeth and me, you would have left him years ago."

"Eva!"

"I have to go; I have work to do."

"I don't know why you're saying such hurtful things. Don't you know this will be alright?"

"Good-bye." I tapped the disconnect button.

I stared at my computer reading lines and seeing nothing. I opened the browser on my personal computer.

There was a yoga class in an hour. I pushed away the papers on my desk, changed and drove to the class.

The studio was filled with older women. There were six of us. One smiled as I walked in. I blinked and looked away and went to the back to get a block. Sweat formed on my skin. The thermometer's blade stood still at one hundred degrees on the back of the wall. I sat in lotus position. My hips ached. I put my hands on my knees. I shifted, putting a block under my butt. I sat taller, my lower back aching. A head-ache was coming on, pain spreading in my shoulders and neck.

A male yoga teacher stood in front. He was one of the owners with his twin sister Jan. "Hi. I'm Doug."

I followed his direction from pose to pose.

I heard his steps walking around the class.

"Drop your shoulders." He placed his hands on either side of my neck. I tried to relax them down but it didn't feel any different. My tears welled up and I widened my eyes keeping them from falling.

He stood behind me, his breath deep.

Soon I was in child's pose. I thought of Michelle. I rocked my forehead side to side, imagining the day's events falling out, the head-ache gone almost as quickly as it had come on.

A couple days later, Mom called.

"Your dad wants this divorce."

"And this is a surprise?"

"After all these years... I put up with too much." Mom cried into the phone. She enunciated each word. "I don't want this divorce."

"You should get a lawyer."

"He said I can keep the house. He isn't touching my teaching pension. He's giving me money from his military pension; I don't need an attorney."

"You can't make decisions like this. You're not thinking straight. Dad did all the finances."

"I'm not getting a divorce."

"You weren't even happy together."

"It was getting better."

"Communicating with notecards wasn't an improvement."

Mom gasped.

"How can you say it was getting better?"

"Your dad and I were separated when you were a toddler. I convinced him to come back. I can do it again."

"What?" A catalogue of memories flew through my mind.

"I can't remember Dad never being there."

"He was at the house when he left for work until you kids went to sleep. I made him stop at the house in the early morning hours. He eventually came back on his own."

I was speechless. "Does Elizabeth know?"

"No."

"Why did you never mention this before?"

"It was better forgotten."

"Why didn't you divorce him when you had the chance?"

"Women didn't do that then. I have kept this family together. He owes me."

"What?"

"When we were living the summer in Mississippi, one time I asked your dad to carry back the laundry to our base housing. Some of the other officers were in the room. I couldn't take that humidity. He took the laundry but didn't say anything. Later when he came home, I was getting dinner ready for the two of us.

Mom paused before speaking. "Your father said, 'Never tell me to do women's work again.'"

My hands cramped holding the phone.

"I have put up with a lot. I will not be divorced."

"You owe yourself to be happy and that's it."

"We were doing fine."

"How can you say that? I found that post-it note on your lampshade."

"What?"

"When I went to pet the orange kitty in your room, I saw that pink note. It said to leave your cats alone, that they're the only things that matter to you that he can't hurt."

Mom didn't answer.

"No, it wasn't getting better." I was louder than I meant.

"Evie, a lot is happening. It's just a note."

"Why won't you walk away when you finally have the chance?"

Mom didn't answer. "No one can ever know about this."

"Why?" My stomach was bloated and I hadn't even eaten.

"It's a family matter."

"Mom, you're not being realistic. I have to go."

"Promise me, Eva."

"Mom, people will find out. Lots of people get divorced. No one will judge you."

Her voice rose. "Not if you tell them."

"I have to go." I hung up.

I sat at my desk determined not to feel anything anymore.

I cracked each one of my knuckles; Mom hated when I did that; she said it caused arthritis, her own fingers becoming knotted. I stared at the screen trying to focus. My face fell in my hands but no tears came.

I picked up the phone to call Gwen. "You said I could call anytime. Is now okay?"

"Of course."

"When my parents were together and I grew up I couldn't fix them."

"It wasn't your job."

"I don't know how to help now. My mom is pretending the divorce isn't going to happen."

Gwen let out an audible sigh. "That's not easy."

"I couldn't figure out how to make them happy when I was younger and I still can't."

"You need to let this go. It's not your job to make them happy. That's on them."

"I don't know. Elizabeth has her family. I have no one."

"That's not true."

"I have to do this. I have to fix them. Michelle would know what to do."

A wave of sadness hit me. I took a deep breath holding back the tears.

"I know you miss her. You'll get through it. You have to take care of you."

"That's not doing enough."

"You need to step away, create some boundaries."

"I have to help my parents."

"This isn't healthy."

"You know, the pain of Michelle was finally fading. She understood the challenges within my family. I don't know how to make my mom understand that this divorce is her opening to freedom. I have to figure this out. I'll help her until she sees that."

"Eva, she might not see divorce like that. It'll be hard for everyone. But you're on your own now and so are they."

~15~

It had been a week since Dad had come for the table. The bruise of that day faded.

Mom chose a lawyer two miles from my parents' house on Thorn Run Road.

When we arrived, the hot summer sun blazed. The short brown cement law office building built in the eighties blasted cold air as we walked in. The hair on my arms stood up. Behind a tall reception desk with oak cabinets behind it, a plump woman wearing glasses on a chain greeted us and took us to meet the attorney, after taking Mom's name, Mary Wyss.

Would Mom revert to her maiden name, Edwards? What would addressing Christmas and birthday cards be? Mrs. Edwards. No, that was Grandma. Miss Edwards? Or would that be Ms. Edwards —?

The receptionist took us into a conference room which was colder than the hallway. I crossed my arms tighter. Mom tugged at her jacket around her shoulders. The chairs looked like they belonged in a library, roomy with side arms and a maroon leather seat. I sat down. Under the table my legs were sealed together.

Mom and I didn't say anything. Her creases of worry looked more defined. Her eyes were red. She sat with her hands folded on her lap.

A yellow notebook lay flat in front of me under my forearms. A pen sat near my hands. Nervous sweat formed in my arm pits.

When the receptionist brought in Sally, the attorney to meet us, she didn't smile; she sized us up and down. She had the build of a gladiator, big and broad across her shoulders in her dress suit and low heels holding up her thick ankles. Her wrinkles and creases landed in a way that looked like she hadn't been happy much of her life.

I forced a smile.

"Has your husband cheated on you?" She demanded.

My eyes went wide; flashes of heat rose in my chest.

"No," Mom answered and pushed away from the table sitting far back in the chair.

"They were married a long time; it didn't work out," I said.

"Where is he living now?" She spat.

"He bought a house in the area." Mom answered. Her eyes were clouded over; she looked small in her chair. The lines in her face drooped in the way of an old woman.

"Sell your house. Get it on the market."

"What? I don't want to move."

"Do it right away."

"No."

Sally looked up and stared at my mom. She brought

her fingers up from the table and slammed them, all her rings hitting hard. "I need a list of his assets."

"We have joint bank accounts."

"What else?"

"Nothing." Mom looked down at the table.

"We have to catch that god-damned bastard." Sally took a drink.

"What other assets does he have? Any foreign accounts?" Sally's hands leaned on the table.

"Edward did the finances."

Sally's gaze shifted to the hand with the bare middle finger. "How can you not have been aware of the money?"

Mom cowered in her chair.

My hands pressed down flat on the table top; my knuckles went white.

"My husband took care of things. That was his role as head of the household." Mom almost whispered.

Sally stood up and dropped a folder in front of Mom. "The Schedule of Fees."

Mom opened the folder, removing two pages of gray paper with legal jargon. The words were big enough to read as I leaned over Mom's shoulder.

"You need to read this and put down a deposit if you want to go forward with my representation."

Mom looked at the paper; her eyes glazed over. My bare arms pressed into hers. The words made no sense.

I looked up from the schedule of fees. "Can you help my mother?"

Sally took a gulp from her ice water, swirling it as she

put it down, the cubes clinking against the glass. "I need a lot more information about the assets. And get that house on the market before coming back."

I stood up from the table. "Dad doesn't have any foreign accounts. And I don't know why you're angry at him — you've never met him."

She looked at me, softening her voice. "Oh I have. I know your father's kind. I'm sick of seeing men pushing women like your mother around."

I looked away from Sally and stared at the wall. Close to my mom, I smelled her sour breath.

Sally wrote in cursive blue letters a list of items that she pushed across the table. "Work on this list."

Mom picked up the paper and stared at the words.

"We'll let you know if my mother decides to work with you." I put my empty cup down on the table.

"Don't take long. There's a lot to prepare."

Mom and I stood, grasping the table and pushing the heavy chairs back.

When we got to my car, Mom opened the front passenger door and sat down. I waited to feel comforted by the black leather seat. I didn't start the car but pushed the button for the windows to go down and the breeze came in, pushing out hot air.

"Thank you, Eve. That was hard."

I stared straight ahead. "It'll be fine, Mom. It always is."

I breathed in deep, knowing the lie I told, tightness rising in my throat and turned on the car. Mom pushed the button for her window to go up and turned on the air conditioning. She never wanted her hair to get messed up.

The distance was short, but felt long.

"At least that appointment is over." I looked ahead at the road.

"Yes."

"She looked like a fighter."

Mom didn't answer.

I wanted to make her laugh by saying she could be a bullfighter, but that was ridiculous.

"I couldn't have done it without you by my side."

I forced a smile and stared straight ahead, the smile gone as soon as it came. "I didn't know the attorney would be like that. Dad can't think that only he can have an attorney; someone needs to represent you."

Mom put her hand on my arm for a quick moment, moved it, sighed and turned away from me, her eyes on the green leafed maple and oak trees going by.

My throat tightened. I blinked hard, glad for my big prescription sunglasses.

We rode the rest of the way in silence.

I parked the car in front of Mom's house and took a deep breath to avoid my voice betraying my weakness. "I have to get back to work. That was my lunch break."

She remained in the car and took my limp and clammy hand.

I looked at Mom unable to offer hope. She let go and got out of the car, much slower than before. She stood on the sidewalk to wave good-bye. I put the passenger side window down.

Mom turned around, leaned into the window. "Eva, maybe you could move back home for a while. I'm not used to being alone."

"Mom, No. You can do this. Let's not think about this right now. A lot happened — I can't. I have my own house. I'm sorry, I —"

Her cheek clenched. Her eyes became glassy. "I thought you were going to take care of me. You said you'd help me."

"Mom, I have my own life. I can't —"

Mom put her hand in the air. She smiled, darkness in her sunken eyes. "Of course you can't. You're busy. Why would you help me?" She turned.

I watched her walk up the steps, waiting for her to unlock the door. She fumbled and turned around, waving for me to leave.

I couldn't speak. I put the window up. I wanted to scream and cry. Nothing came out. My foot hit the accelerator and at the stop sign before turning onto the highway, I rang Gwen's phone.

"I don't understand why my parents have been together all this time. I don't know why Mom keeps choosing Dad when he keeps hurting her."

"You'll never know."

"Today my mom asked me to move back home."

"You told her no; didn't you?" Gwen's voice rose.

"Yes, of course. It made me feel awful. But I can't imagine —"

"And don't. Remember what I said about boundaries."

"Yes, but she's my mother. Why did she spend so long pretending they were happy?"

"She did the best she could. We all do."

"When I was a toddler my parents were separated. My mom made my dad be at the house when we woke up and went to bed; they've been pretending a long time."

Gwen drew in her breath. "This divorce will happen. It's going to be hard."

"I couldn't stand up for Michelle; I had to obey; I had to be fine with every decision from when she died. I didn't speak up at her funeral. I hated the pain I carried with me then, being silent. It's happening all over again, but I can't pretend anymore. I'm not doing it."

"No one says you have to. And you're not. You're speaking up about it now and telling your mom no about moving back in says you're living in the reality. You're speaking your truth."

I was silent. Then I spoke. "I better go. I'm still driving. Thanks for those words. It's hard to believe those things right now. Maybe I will sometime. I just don't know." I gripped the steering wheel.

"Believe me, I know. Call me anytime."

My shoulders and neck ached; my usual headache was coming on as I maneuvered steep hills and bends. I drove home, arriving ten minutes faster than usual.

In my bedroom I changed into yoga clothes, grabbed my mat and went straight to the studio. I waited an hour on a bench outside until class started and walked in, finding a spot in the back away from everyone. And as before, Doug put his hands on my shoulders, melting away some tension.

Closing my eyes in shavasana, Michelle's face floated in my mind, her wavy strawberry blond hair falling behind her. Her face was tight, like the day we fought in the gallery. My cheeks burned as hot tears came.

~16~

Two days later, I called Gwen.

"My dad called. He wants me to see his new house and then have lunch."

"Go. You can leave if it gets tough."

"He's the one who started all this. I don't want to go there."

"The sooner you go, the better it'll be."

"I doubt that."

"When are you seeing him?"

"Today in an hour, less than that, since we're on the phone."

"You better get ready."

"I'll never be."

"Eva, you can do this."

"I feel guilty about encouraging Mom to get the lawyer. But she never would've without me and she asked me to move back in. I can't. I told her that. You should have seen her face. I still love Dad, but he would be angry if he knew I was helping her. He's my dad and he's not perfect. But we've had good times together, too. I love him. I help one parent and I hurt the other. I can't win. When is this going to end?"

"Eva, take a couple deep breaths. You'll get through this."

"It's hard."

"I know. See your Dad. It might help."

"Maybe." I hung up the phone, ran up the stairs to grab my purse and keys, put on my navy flip-flops and headed out. All the windows went down in the car, even though my hair blew all over. The warm sun streamed in the car. After I got off the highway and onto the backroads, I drove the familiar way past the ice cream place and onto the orange belt. I went a different way to not pass Mom's house on Blackburn Road. I drove past Mom's attorney's office. I swallowed hard on a knot of phlegm that came up. My belly bulged with the anxious bloat growing in my stomach.

I drove slower, dropping gears, past my grandparents' house; they had both passed away.

I turned from Fern Hollow to Scaife Road past the white picketed fences where a couple horses grazed, up and down the steep hill that my mom said she rode her bike with no hands as a kid. I took the left on Merriman Road, Dad's street. I pulled in the gravel driveway in front of the detached garage. I sat there a minute, not moving. My stomach gurgled.

Dad came out of the house and the storm door slammed. "Eva."

I turned my head and waved through the window. I opened the door and stood up.

"Want a tour of my house?"

My shoulders slumped. "Right. Hi, Dad." I faked being cheerful.

I went to hug him and he held on longer. I wore my big sunglasses. Past Dad's shoulder, I saw his garden.

Dad opened the storm door and held it for me. The entry door was already open.

"Don't you lock the doors?"

"There's no reason to."

"But your house abuts the woods."

"It's safe here," Dad answered.

I looked at him not knowing what to say.

"Here's the living room."

I coughed. "What's that musty smell?"

"I thought it was gone. An old woman lived here before."

"Maybe you could try opening some windows."

"I did that."

"Check for mold. What came up in your inspection?" I coughed again. "That smell is horrible!"

"That's a waste of money." Dad's eyebrows furrowed.

"You didn't do an inspection?"

"I didn't need one."

At my parents' house lemon-scented wood polish wafted through the house.

To my left the dark medieval German pictures hung on neutral walls.

"You should put some color on these drab walls."

Dad didn't answer.

"That's a new couch." I pointed to the long one to my right. "It's big."

"One of my friends gave it to me."

"Oh." I stared at it. The long one at home Mom had refabricated a number of times; they'd brought it back from the Philippines.

"We come from big people."

"Dad, I know."

He laughed. "I guess I told you that one a few times."

In front of the couch was the long rosewood coffee table that my parents had bought when Dad was stationed overseas.

In the middle was the blue leather chair, that my cat Sam ruined. Mom had complained that I owed her $400. Next to the blue chair was the chess table, where Dad taught my sister and me how to play. He always told us when we made good moves. Once or twice, I'd beaten him.

"Evie," Dad called.

I looked up lost in the days of chess playing. "What?"

"The kitchen." Dad displayed his hand out as he ducked his head, nearly whacking it on the hanging stained glass light.

"Right." I took a step and peered straight ahead.

That kitchen needed updates and had little natural light, only one small window on a wall behind the refrigerator and a side door looking out to the garden. To the right of the counter stood that familiar kitchen table. A sharp cramp in my belly made me wince.

"Are you coming?" He walked ahead of me down the hall.

"Yeah."

He pointed. "Bathroom."

It was a full one, dirty, like Dad kept it at my parents'.

Dad took a few more steps. "Bedroom." He pointed again.

The bed had the familiar walnut headboard and a sag on the left side where Dad had slept when my parents were together. Here he slept on the right, Mom's place, judging from the impression on the pillow and the Eisenhower book on a slant on the nightstand.

"And my office." Dad turned in the opposite direction.

Stuff was all over the desk. Programming and computer books lined the shelf. A set of tall freestanding shelves was next to his squeaky wooden chair.

"It's small."

Dad shrugged.

"Does the house have a fireplace?"

"No."

"I bet you'll miss that."

"Yes. Are you ready to go?"

"I'm not feeling well. Can we go another time?"

My shoulders and neck were killing me. A headache threatened.

"Why didn't you tell me before?" Dad's voice rose.

"I thought it would go away. My stomach feels bad and my head hurts."

"You must have the miseries."

In our family that was code for getting sick.

He looked at me like he was looking for something else. "Do you have a fever?" He walked toward me.

I took a step back. "No, Dad. I'm gonna go. Sorry about today."

"We can eat Italian another time." He walked over to hug me.

I put up my hand. "I might be sick."

"Right." He put one hand in his shorts pocket.

"I'm going now." I waved and headed for the door.

Dad's disappointment drifted behind me as the screen door slammed. I almost ran to my car. As I pulled out, Dad stood outside the doorway. His shoulders slumped forward; he wasn't standing tall and proud like he usually did. I put up my hand to wave.

My car sped around the curves of the street. I drove fast, turning hard on the bends. My neck pain was sharp. I slouched down into the seat, breathing out deeply like the yoga teachers always said to do. The windows were down. Hot tears came down my face. Once I crossed the intersection away from Dad's, I pulled over at an Arby's and put my head in my hands. I wiped my arm across my face and put the car back in drive.

I put the windows up and called Gwen.

"Is this a good time?" The words fell out of my mouth.

"Sure. You're not with your Dad?"

"No. He gave me the tour; then I left. My nerves got to me."

Gwen's silence comforted me.

"Why do I still feel like that kid between them?"

"You don't have to be."

"They need me and I have to stay strong; I'm faking it. I have to suck it up no matter how much it hurts. It's my duty to help them. What was even real between my parents? I should've moved away like Elizabeth did."

"You don't have to pretend anything."

I wiped my tears away with the back of my hand.

"This is never going to end." A flash of heat rose from my chest to my face.

The line was quiet.

"Gwen, are you still there?"

"Yes. There's no right way of getting through this. Try to take it a day at a time. Don't look back to how things were."

"The past led up to this."

"Yes, but looking back is hurting you."

~17~

The following Saturday morning, I called Dad.
"Sorry about last weekend. You like Thai. Can we meet at the Green Mango, the one near my house?"

"What time?"

"12:00? I'll meet you there."

"Okay, Evie-kins."

"'Kay, Dad."

He was inside sitting on the bench waiting and stood up to embrace me.

Dad's bear hugs expressed all that words couldn't.

"Thanks for not squeezing the life out of me, Dad." A nervous laugh escaped me.

Dad looked down, a smile on his face.

We sat. Dad had his vegetarian green curry and I had my usual pineapple curry.

"So, what's new?" I asked.

Dad frowned. "Your mother and that damned attorney of hers are dragging this out."

My face burned hot.

"This wouldn't be happening if she'd gotten rid of those cats. She has eighteen of them and leaves food for strays. It attracts raccoons. There was a deer on the porch. I told her to get rid of them and she wouldn't. I had no choice but to give her those divorce papers."

Sweat formed on my lip. I drank my glass of water as I remembered the attorney's mantra, "we're going to take him down."

"This isn't happening because of the cats, Dad. Mom is a part of me, just as much as you. Don't talk about her like that. It hurts."

Dad stopped chewing his food, staring at me.

"She's keeping me from ending our marriage with that — dragon lady she's hired."

I eyed the door, wishing I could run away. Tears that weren't going to fall filled my eyes. Tightness rose in my shoulders.

"Mom needs someone to represent her. Do you really think she would agree with everything you're dishing out — especially after all you've put her through?"

Dad's eyes widened as he stared at me. His palms landed hard and fast on the table; the silverware and plates stirred.

Dad's voice rose. "She can keep the house; she'll have access to my pension. She's getting a good offer."

The hum of the restaurant stopped; eyes turned toward us.

"Mom never should've settled for you. Your drinking ruined everything good that could have happened to our family."

Dad's face went crimson. He put down his fork and looked at me. "Elizabeth knew when to be quiet."

I stared back; my ears burned. "I'm not pretending that your alcoholism doesn't exist anymore." Tears flowed down my face.

"I chose to drink. I needed a break from your mother's nagging and when I lost my job, and — it's not how you're making it sound. You're twisting my words, just like your mother."

"Your drinking destroyed our family. Mom stayed with you. She wanted to keep the family together. God knows why. You think she deserves what you've done to her?"

"You don't know your mother."

"She kept us together. Yes, that's right. When you lost your job, it was her teaching income that kept us afloat. You never appreciated everything she did. She tried to encourage us when you put us down. You still don't see everything she did."

"She kept me from getting that promotion in New York. I missed opportunities because of her. A woman's job is to stay at home, take care of the kids. She defied me. My career could have been — Yes, I drank. It's not what you call it. I was — unwinding."

My muscles were tight. I stared him down.

Dad's lips pursed tight and he flattened his palms on the table.

A solid minute went by.

"You'll never understand what I've put up with from your mother. She didn't belong in the job market. It was her responsibility to raise the family, to do the women's work — "

"Dad, you talk like it's the 1950s. It's not. It's way past that now.

Dad bristled but didn't answer.

"How many times did I ask you to watch movies with us? I tried to keep us together, to keep the conversation moving. You chose that repulsive red jug instead."

"I needed a break. I didn't want to think."

I wiped the tears off my face. I stared at the pineapples and rice on my plate. Then I looked up seeing people I didn't know staring at us, pity on their faces. Some looked away, or at each other, shaking their heads.

I started out with a lower voice. "If you had once admitted your drinking was a problem; I mean, really gotten help, asked for it and tried, God, Dad, that would've been, — well, of course you didn't do that. We wouldn't be here if you had admitted you were the problem. No, it was easier to blame everyone else. God forbid, you admitted weakness. Mom would've been proud of you even after everything she did to cover up your drinking problem, your alcoholism." I spat out the words.

Dad's eyes narrowed at me. His silence I had grown used to. For once it didn't unhinge me, make me nauseated or walk away.

I kept talking and faced him for all those years I didn't. "If you had just gotten help, all that she had done for you would've been worth it — You might have treated her — with respect. Instead, you blame her; you still do, finding excuses — the cats. Oh, it's the eighteen cats' —that don't exist. God, Dad. Do you think we're that stupid?

Do you think we haven't lived long enough knowing what has really broken this family? Everything she did for you was for nothing. I needed to see the father who fell down, asked for help and did the work to end addiction, or whatever it took. Instead, anything bad that happened became Mom's fault. It wasn't fair what you did to her, — or to us, as a family."

Voices around us stopped. Metal clinked on dishes every now and then.

Dad's face was red; his eyes were wide. "Evie, settle down." Dad's voice was controlled and loud.

I stared back at Dad, no longer holding my tears. They streamed down.

My voice broke. "Dad, we wanted you to fall so you'd stop drinking. We needed you to realize what was happening. We, — I wanted to stop pretending everything was fine. I needed to see you face your drinking problem. I wanted a dad who turned to us."

My hand covered my face as I sobbed, my shoulders shaking.

Dad's voice lowered, softened even. "Evie, That's not —" He started and then stopped.

He dropped his stare from my burning face and picked up his utensils. He shoved rice and green sauce on his fork. He stared away from me. I looked at my plate and wanted to eat as much as possible. I fixed my gaze to the door.

My eyes returned to Dad, his head down.

"You wouldn't be divorcing Mom if you'd just faced it and moved on. We wouldn't be here." I pleaded.

Dad's voice was barely above a whisper. "I gave your mother those divorce papers to spare her. I'll never be able to fix everything she wanted from me. I can't stop drinking."

~18~

I traveled for work that week. Mom had reached out many times; I let the calls go to voicemail. I was on the phone with Mom the following weekend. I sat back on my couch.

"Your father needs me. What if he has an accident? What if he gets another DUI?"

"What? How many has he had?"

"Two."

"When did this happen?"

"Before you were born. And then later."

"Why did you stay with Dad?"

"A woman's role is to be loyal to her husband and keep the family together."

"Why did you let him drink?"

"You don't understand." Her voice broke.

I listened to her cry until she blew her nose and starting talking again.

"Do you remember when your dad chose his drinking over us when you kids were living at home?"

Of course I remembered. "Please stop talking." My words came out fast and loud knowing where this led.

My mother continued as if in a trance. "When we

lived in Mississippi I had to pick him up from his com-
mander's, who'd kept him from the base jail. Edward had
been in a drunken stupor near the officer's club in Biloxi;
he'd passed out; I had to change him from his urinated-
stained clothes. I don't know why you love your dad, why
you still see him after everything. Maybe now you'll be
on my side. Please move back home, Evie. I need you.
Elizabeth is busy with her family. You have no one and
you're here. It's your responsibility to help me through
this and help me hide what's happening. I don't want
to work with that lawyer. This marriage doesn't have to
end."

"Stop it." I shouted.

It all came back in a flurry of broken scenes: Dad holding onto the rail, the slow ascent up the steps, getting
Dad the glass of water, the sound of glass and water hitting the hardwood floor as I heard the pee hitting the wall
where it met the fireplace.

Hot angry tears let loose. My face burned. My hands
cramped tight as I held the phone. I couldn't breathe.

"I have to go, Mom. I can't listen to this; I can't pretend hard things don't happen anymore." My voice rose
loud and fast. I clicked off the phone before she had a
chance to respond. I ran to the bathroom; hot liquid
surged up. Vomit and tears mixed together as I clung to
the toilet. The memories kept flashing in my mind: Dad
turning, "Evie, what are you doing?"

Behind Dad, I saw the wet stain darkening the beige
wall.

I tried to remember the next day after that and was blank. I couldn't remember ever talking about it or thinking of it before now. I sat up on the edge of the bathtub and stared ahead, tears mixed in with snot; my throat burning from throwing up. I blinked hard trying not to remember anything from that night.

-19-

D ear Mom,

I can't be the person you talk to about the divorce. You pretend that Dad isn't an alcoholic; it horrifies me. You act like everything is going to be fine, but it isn't. Stop pretending it's going to work out with him. I don't understand why you protect him after all these years. I tried to help you in getting that lawyer so you could stand up to him, but I can't do anything else anymore. He is my father and I love him. Being in the middle of your divorce hurts too much. I know your friends will listen, but I can't and I won't. If you start complaining about him, I will leave or I will hang up.

Eva

~ 20 ~

A month passed after my last contacts with Mom and Dad. I received angry emails from Mom, and I created a folder with her name on it and filed them away like they never appeared.

In that time, I had kept up with my yoga, I met Gwen for coffees and at some point during those days, I met Karl, a tall and blond German post-doc scientist on cross-country skis at a Pittsburgh meetup two hours away. We enjoyed many of the same outdoor activities. As it got warmer, we shared new discoveries like fishing. I'd never rowed a boat before. One time we did that.

One day we went hiking at Moraine State Park, north of Pittsburgh. After that, he took me to a European bakery on the North Side of town.

Karl spoke German to the owner. They both laughed and she looked at me. Karl put his arm around my shoulder and brought me closer.

I looked up at him.

She handed him the white box and gave him his change.

We walked over to the stone benches and sat down across from each other. Karl opened the box.

I took out one of the Napoleons. "What did you say?"

"I told her how we met skiing north of here." He reached into his pocket.

"What's this?"

He pushed a small blue velvet box toward me. "I saw this and thought of you."

I raised my eyebrows and looked at him. "Karl—"

"Open it."

Inside the box held a necklace with a shell stone inside a silver setting. "It's beautiful." I held it in my hand, looked at it and then at him.

"I noticed that when you wear that bracelet that you don't have a necklace to match. I thought you'd like this."

I leaned over and hugged him. "Karl, Thank you."

I left to pickup Karl before meeting Gwen at the German brewery. He carried a couple beer bottles to the recycling bin before getting in my car.

"Drinking already?"

"Loosen up, babe. I was drinking to unwind."

"Is there something wrong?"

He clicked his tongue.

"We're meeting Gwen for pretzels and beer soon."

"You worry about you. I'll take care of me."

I looked at him and drove to the brewery.

A small chortle escaped from him.

"What's funny?"

"Nothing. I was thinking of something in German. It's hard to translate."

"Hmm."

I continued driving until we arrived; Karl looking out the window without speaking.

Upon arriving and meeting Gwen, he drank more than usual. The conversation was light and mostly Gwen and I talked, Karl occasionally adding a comment. When the bill came Karl grabbed it.

When we left, he put his arms around me and kissed my cheek. We said our goodbyes to Gwen and walked to the car. As usual, Karl opened the car door for me before going to his, even though I drove. He sang traditional German songs. That night we went to see a band playing at Club Café.

The next day I met Gwen for coffee at Big Dog. The shop was in an old building, with high ceilings and an old wooden mantle. A fireplace cracked wood embers in the corner where two cushioned wicker rocking chairs faced each other. We both sat down in them, empty for a change.

Gwen spread out her hands on the table. "Was everything okay yesterday?"

"What do you mean?" I sat forward in my chair.

"Karl didn't say much."

"He's a scientist; he's quiet." I could feel Gwen's eyes as I looked down at my mug while stirring the cream.

"Did I show you the necklace he gave me?" I picked up the pendant under my shirt. "It's pretty; isn't it? I would've showed you yesterday but Karl would've objected like I was bragging. Sometimes he's moody."

Gwen looked at it. "It is nice. Pay attention to how he treats you."

"So far mostly good. He was talking about his work visa earlier."

"What do you mean?"

"There's a deadline to get it extended; it expires soon. There's a lottery to apply for the green card. He was probably thinking about that."

"Are you sure you want to get closer to him? He might leave."

"Gwen, it's fine. I can't be worried about whether he leaves or not. Right now he's here and I'm enjoying him."

"There are a lot of men here in Pittsburgh who aren't leaving."

I sat on the couch, getting ready to watch a sci-fi thriller Karl had found online.

He sat down next to me, joining me under the blanket. He put the wooden bowl of popcorn on the coffee table in front of us. "When am I going to meet your parents?"

My neck hair stood up. "What's the hurry?"

He shrugged. "You said they live here. You hardly talk about them."

"I don't need to. I have my own life now. We're not close."

"Is there anything you want to tell me?" He squeezed my shoulder.

"Like what?"

"Is there something I should know?"

I shook my head. "No, not really." I leaned back into his chest and settled my head against him. He put his arm around me and with the other pushed play.

As the time passed, we did most things together when I wasn't on the road doing sales visits. When I came home from my business trips, he always made sure there were flowers on the table. He often cooked. When he won movie tickets through a work raffle, it was me he took. Much of the time we spent at my house. Sometimes he worked late in the lab. Our time apart left me time to do my own things and when we were together again, it was like we were never apart. He was full of discovery often wanting to learn more. He took me to his work parties, introducing me to his colleagues.

One time he was on Skype with his parents and he called me to join him for a quick hello. His dad was much older than my father with a full head of white hair. Wrinkles creased his forehead, crows' feet rooted around his eyes. Lines planted around his mouth where the laugh lines belonged. Peter was retired though I didn't know from what. Karl never mentioned. His mother, Martina worked from home teaching piano. I stood behind Karl who was seated at the small table in my kitchen. I knelt down seeing his parents. Happiness danced between them; their eyes smiled when they talked. A knot grew in my throat seeing what they had together. I blinked it away, smiled, said a quick hello and made an excuse to get away.

That night, Karl and I made dinner together. It was routine at my house. I made the salad. He made the main dish. He drank his beer while we cooked. Usually he didn't drink until we'd eaten.

"Anything wrong?" I asked once he threw his can in the recycling bin.

His eyes met mine. "I could say the same to you. Why did you walk away the first time of meeting my parents on Skype?"

"I wasn't ready. I wanted to look better."

"That's stupid. I wanted you to meet them; they've been asking about you. Why haven't I met yours?"

"My parents aren't like yours."

"What?"

"I don't mean that in a bad way. I don't like talking about them."

"You never talk about them. We have a lot of fun together. But why don't you ever talk about your family?"

I braved a smile, put my hand on his chest and pushed him away. "Karl, stop, you're being ridiculous. Stop badgering me." I faked a laugh.

"You're doing it again. Changing the subject."

"Karl. I'm tired. I don't want to talk about this."

"What do you not want me to know?"

"Nothing. Just forget it, okay? Your parents look happy together."

"Ja. They've always been. Sure they've had their moments. But they're happy. They always will be." He shrugged.

"Hmm. That's nice." My voice was quiet. I didn't offer anything more. We talked through dinner, light and casual.

By the end of dinner, I noticed Karl's fifth beer can in the recycling.

"Why are you drinking so much tonight?"

He looked at me but didn't answer. He took his plate to the sink, scraped the food off and put it in the dishwasher. Not saying a word, he took two more cans and disappeared into the living room. I heard the TV turn on. I stared at the cans in the bin.

I shook my head and bit my lip. I put away my dish, walked past Karl and went upstairs.

In the morning while Karl slept, I slipped away to meet Gwen at the gym. After class we had our traditional smoothies.

"What's wrong? You've hardly said anything today."

I picked at my cuticle. "Karl drank a lot yesterday. We were at home. Probably it was nothing and I'm overreacting."

"What happened?"

I filled her in. "There was no reason for him to drink that much." I finished.

I told you before. "If there's any doubt, back out."

I shrugged. "It was probably nothing. It hasn't happened in a while. It's probably my fault. I don't want to tell him what's going on with my parents. He asked again. I met his parents on Skype. They looked so happy; it made me want to cry."

Gwen tilted her head. "Karl would understand if you told him."

I shook my head. "My parents are so different than his. Just in a couple of minutes I saw their love for each other. It — hurt me. I know Karl wanted me to stay and talk to them. I made something up and walked away. I don't want Karl to know how I'm — I don't know — so damaged."

"He wouldn't think that. But it doesn't mean he has to drink like that either. You need to think about that."

I nodded. "I gotta go. Karl should be up now."

"Sure, you're okay?"

"Yeah, sure. Why wouldn't I be? I'm overreacting. It's nothing."

"Your mom used to say that."

"This isn't the same thing. Really, I have to go."

As the months passed, we didn't talk about his visa expiring soon. I didn't talk about my parents either. I didn't worry about what came next.

I continued to ignore contact made from both of my parents as they continued to badmouth each other as the months passed. It didn't exist anymore. I decided it was time to be happy; they had their lives. I was growing mine now with Karl; I would tell him about my parents. But not now.

～21～

I stood in the entryway of Karl's apartment; it was rare to be at his place; often he came to mine. The door was wide open. A few boxes had been put together. Cleaned plates piled high next to the sink. Clothing sat folded in a corner. Tidy papers and textbooks lay in several different spots on the floor near his feet. A clay brown curtain draped across the front window. Karl lay against an oversized pillow on the orange couch and watched a movie.

"Shouldn't you be packing?"

"What?" He turned his head. "Oh, hey, Eve.'"

"Did you forget your lease is expiring at the end of the day?"

"My friends bailed. Finish watching this with me. I'll make us some lunch and then we can get to it."

"What about the rental truck?"

"I haven't picked it up; I was waiting for you." He pointed.

"How are you going to get everything done? It's getting close to rush hour. We have to pack up everything and take it to my place."

He shrugged. "You can drive with me. You know the shortcuts."

"You should've been packing earlier. You've known this was coming for a month."

"Eva. Come on." He stood behind me and rubbed my shoulders. I didn't move. He kissed my neck. "This is hard."

I stepped away from his touch. "Why didn't you find a way to extend your visa? Everyone else on your team got the green card but you."

"We've been through this before."

"Karl, it should've been easy for you."

"It's like a lottery; the chances to get it are slim."

"Why didn't you try? The others did."

"Don't start."

"You say it like I don't mean anything to you."

"That's not what I meant and you know it." He took my hand in his.

"You don't care whether you stay or go. Where does that put us?"

"Eva, you're twisting this around. It wasn't possible to stay and even if I did, the grant for my funding was going to run out. Where could I work without a sponsor? No company wants to pay for all that."

"But it hasn't run out. You've just decided it would. Why didn't you try?"

"Eva! This conversation is a waste of time. We've been through it before. It's too late to change anything." He stood up heading to the bathroom.

"If you could go back and change things, would you?"

The water in the sink was running. He opened the door, his hands still wet and wiped them with a towel hanging by the sink.

"This conversation doesn't change anything." He stepped out of the bathroom and back in the kitchen.

We stood apart.

"Nothing I did was going to change our situation."

"You could've tried."

"Do you know how much paper work there is? And with no income, how was that going to work?"

"I could support you until you found something."

"I can't be here without a work visa." He grabbed me with his arms and held me close. He looked down at me. "You know how I feel about you. But I can't change this—" He let me go and put his hands out. "This funding, this problem with the Visa. I can't fix any of this. You have no idea how bad it feels."

"Actually I do." I bit my lip and looked at the floor.

He took my hands down at my side. He hugged me. "I'm sorry, Eva." His voice was muffled; his mouth spoke into my hair.

I stepped away from him. "We better go get the truck."

He grabbed his stuff and we left.

I met Gwen for lunch later that week. We'd met for Mexican on East Carson Street on the corner.

"How'd the move go?" She picked up her drink.

I shook my shoulders. "We got through it. It wasn't easy."

"When does he leave?"

"In three weeks." I took a big bite of the mole sauce in my burrito.

"You're not going to keep in touch with him, right? I mean, long distance? How's it ever going to work?"

I shrugged. "This visa stuff could be temporary. We don't know what's going to happen. Anyway, I'm going to visit him soon for a month. Maybe he'll find a job in not long and I can join him."

"You'd really leave just like that? You've barely been together six months."

I clenched my fork. "We're adults. We know what we want. I've seen enough of him to know."

"Did you tell him about your parents yet?"

"I don't want to ruin it by bringing up that stuff."

"You haven't been in touch with them?"

"I'm finally happy with Karl. They made their own mess. They need to clean it up. I can't deal with all that anymore."

"Do you think Karl is telling you everything?"

"Why wouldn't he? Look, my mother knew about my dad's drinking from the beginning of their marriage. She stayed with him for what? For the sake of keeping together our family? There's a good reason people get divorced these days. My parents should've done it years ago. Karl and I are happy. It's tricky right now but we'll make it work."

Gwen sat back in her chair. Her plate was empty. "I don't think this is a situation you want to be in."

"Things aren't always easy. We'll figure it out."

"You should tell him about your parents."

"There's no reason to. He likes me the way I am. Who knows what he'll think of me if I talk about all that. Besides my parents' stuff happened before Karl and I met. There's no reason to bring it up."

"Don't you think he'll feel cut out? Like you didn't think he was important enough?"

"Why are we even talking about this? You were the one who said I should end it with him."

"If you're going to be with him, you have to be able to tell him the hard stuff. You can't dance around pretending bad things don't happen."

"Gwen, I know. I spent most of life doing that growing up. I don't want to talk about this anymore."

She shook her head.

I stood at the curb and watched him pull out the luggage, his red bike that looked like a ten speed and the flattened bike box. "Why didn't you assemble that at my house?"

"The box has to be assembled here at the airport for security reasons."

I stared at him with my hand on my hip.

"Go on the website and check."

"I have to move the car before they ticket me."

"You're going to see me off?"

I pointed to the window outside. "I was going to drive to short term parking."

He looked up.

"Are you going to pack the bike in time?"

"Ja."

"It's an international flight! I told you we would be late."

He ignored me and bent two sides of the box.

"I'm going."

"You're coming back?"

"I said I would. You better get your ass in gear."

"I-am-working-on-it." He stood up, his sweaty lips in a tight line. He turned away and folded up another side of the box. His muscles flexed when he picked up the bike frame.

"I hope you figure that out."

He stood up, towering over me. "Eva, I'd be able to do this if you didn't keep bossing me around; I know this isn't easy for you."

I crossed my arms ignoring the knot forming in my throat. I let out a loud sigh.

"I know it doesn't seem like it, but it's going to work out for us." He looked down at me, his face tight, the lines around his mouth sagging more than usual.

"I'll see you at check-in." I backed away and slid into the seat of my car.

I saw him at the ticket counter, talking with the long haired blond gate agent.

"Karl, it's almost time for your flight."

"Eva." He squeezed my shoulder like nothing bad ever happened between us.

I half-smiled. "Did you get the bike packed in time?"

He pointed. "Ja."

It passed on the conveyor belt behind the agent.

"Good."

He heaved his bulging luggage on the weighing machine. I looked at his back as he heaved up his suitcase.

We watched the red numbers. Ninety-eight pounds.

"What did you pack in there?"

"I couldn't leave everything at your house."

"$175." The agent announced.

"Bags are free on international flights," Karl corrected.

"Not when they're over the weight limit."

"Right." He forked over his credit card to the agent.

He turned to me.

"You better go. You need to be at the gate in forty minutes. There's still security downstairs." I pointed to the escalators behind us.

He kissed me in an embrace. His bangs flopped in his eyes and I moved them away, putting my hand on his cheek. "I miss you already."

"Eva, I want you to know that — "

"Go," the gate agent hollered.

He turned.

"Run!" I watched him take big steps away with his backpack swinging.

He turned around watching me until the escalator went down and I could no longer see him.

-22-

A couple days later, Gwen and I met for coffee in the neighboring town. We sat outside; Gwen's basset hound Hazel lay under the table.

The sun warmed my skin. I picked up my cappuccino.

Gwen sat across from me as Hazel settled down in the shade.

I set down my white mug. "Just because my parents can't find happiness doesn't mean I can't."

"There are other men in this city." Gwen shifted her foot away from Hazel.

"We're in a rough spot. We'll make it through this. I'll be pleasantly surprised."

"He's not here anymore. Why should you uproot your life? He didn't do anything to stay." Gwen's voice dripped with doubt.

"We'll work this out. Karl is a good man; we have fun together. He was busy with his deadlines so he didn't have enough time for the visa application extension."

"Why do you insist on keeping this relationship? He's not even on the same continent anymore. And you never told him about your parents' situation. This relationship is not just about him." Gwen dipped her biscotti in her latté.

"Every relationship has hard times. This is ours. Besides, look at my parents — "

"It shouldn't be hard this early on," Gwen interrupted.

"Giving up is failing. My dad always said that. It'll be different with Karl and me. My parents will see that I can have a good relationship even though they can't."

"That's a horrible reason." Gwen widened her fingers on the table.

"I need to know I tried."

"You're setting yourself up." Gwen sighed.

"Long term relationships mean compromise; you know that. You've been married."

"You gotta let this one go." Gwen dipped the last of her cookie in her mug.

I fingered the necklace he'd given me.

Gwen sipped from her mug. "How are you really dealing with knowing he didn't try to stay here? You argued a lot before he left."

"Gwen, really, it's fine. I'll use my yoga breathing." I tried to laugh.

"You're going to need more than that." Gwen pushed her mug away.

"He owes me a great vacation."

"What do you mean he owes you?"

"He'll see how much I helped him before he left and want to return the favor."

"That's crazy. You can't expect that to happen. You'll

be paying for it and then I will." She muttered as her chair screeched back.

"I heard that."

"Go to Europe without him; Ireland is nice this time of year."

"You're supposed to be my supportive friend."

"I'm not going to pretend that you should be with him. You didn't even feel comfortable enough to tell him about your parents' divorce." Gwen picked up her drink to finish it.

"Look, it's going to be fine. This relationship is one thing I can control in my life that's going to go right."

"You're not thinking —I know your parents' divorce has been hard — " Gwen started.

Hazel who was lying under the table stood up and barked, staring right at me.

Gwen and I laughed.

Her smile disappeared. "Even Hazel knows you need to end it."

"I didn't know your dog could bark."

"She only barks when it's important."

I took a big gulp from my lukewarm cappuccino. "It'll be fine. I can't help the visa situation. It's over now. We argued because of that. That's all it is." I looked down at my fingers as I spread them out on the table.

"If you and he were so close, why didn't you ever tell him about your parents and how hard it's been?"

"I didn't want to. That stuff is hard. I didn't want him to feel bad, or, pity me."

"If you can't talk to him about that, how can you expect this to work out?"

"Life doesn't have to be about all the hard things."

I felt Gwen's stare but couldn't meet her eyes.

～23～

Two days later on the weekend, Mom called. I took the call despite not having spoken to her since the silence started over six months ago.

"Eva, where have you been?"

"I told you in the emails, Mom; I've been busy with work; I travel every week."

"I want to see you."

"I'm not sure." My heart raced.

"Are you going to be there?"

"Yes, but if you're going to be talking about the divorce, then, no, I don't want you to come."

"I never brought it up. I'll be there in twenty minutes."

I paused, not sure if I could believe her because all the emails she'd been sending were the opposite.

"Alright."

"I'll be there soon."

My jeans became tight as my stomach bloated as I clicked the phone. My armpits dampened under my shirt.

I opened the door and she walked through the house into the kitchen.

"Your father makes me angry." She held the pop can in her hand and moved the glass on the counter.

"I told you I'm not doing this. You said you wouldn't talk about this before coming here."

She ignored me and kept talking. "Your dad and I were doing fine. We even shared a few laughs before he moved out."

I took the glass from the counter and put it back in the cabinet. I stood in front of her, hands on my hips. "You have to go. I told you I can't do this. Did you even read my letter?"

"That letter was offensive. I can't do this by myself. You have to help me. Move in with me. No one will miss you here."

"Mom, I have my own life here; I'm not moving back home. You said he was letting you keep the house and you wanted that." I tried to breathe. My lips sweat.

"I can't stand being alone all day."

I gasped. "Talk to your friends. You'll feel better in your own home soon. It takes time getting used to it."

Mom shook her head. "I can't get used to it. I won't." She crossed her arms.

"I have my own life."

"You should be helping me. I supported you when you lived at home."

"This isn't the same thing."

"I don't like being alone."

"You practically were when Dad was there. You both lived separate lives. Sell the house like the lawyer said. You can live in that fifty-five plus community. You'll meet people there."

"I don't want to be around all those old people."

Mom shook her head. "I can make him come back. He'll never make it on his own without me. Stay with me until he comes back."

I shook my head. "Mom, you'll get through this. Stop pretending he's coming back. He's not going to."

"I cleared out your old room so you can move back in. What you're doing to me is mean. Just like your father."

"No! It's not even the same thing. I have my own house."

"You need to choose a side. Remember how bad he made you feel."

I gasped and took a deep breath. "He's my father. He is flawed, maybe deeply. But I love him. He gave us some good memories, those family outings, like you have."

"Your father has some problems. I kept this family together. I bailed him out countless times."

"I know, Mom. And it hurt our family. You weren't happy."

"I did it for the family."

"Dad won't change his mind. You need to accept that this divorce is happening."

I left Mom in the kitchen and walked to the door.

She followed me. "I can't believe you're doing this to me. How can you take his side?"

"I told you this before; I don't want to talk about this; this is your problem with Dad. It's upsetting that you're asking me to choose you or Dad. I can't and I won't do it."

The wrinkle lines tensed on her face. "You want to know what's upsetting? When your own daughter who has no life of her own won't help me."

"I got you the attorney, Mom. I went with you. You have a chance to stand up for yourself. But you won't." I frowned.

She took a step forward, standing closer to me. "And what did that do? She's expensive and I don't even need her. I fired her."

"Mom! Things are never going to change with you and Dad. Why can't you see that?"

"I'll get your father to listen. We aren't going to be a divorced family. I'll make this work."

"Please leave." I opened the door.

Mom stopped at the entrance and turned around, pointing her finger at me. "My own daughter won't stay by my side."

"It hurts me when you say this is what you want." I put my hand on the door knob to close it.

She stepped back onto the porch. "Other people shouldn't see things fall apart. This family doesn't have to."

"You had a choice to leave. You threatened to divorce him before. Why do you keep pretending?"

"Eva, why are you angry? I'm the one dealing with this divorce. You run all over the country making work excuses when you don't feel like being responsible to me." Mom's eyes were glassy.

I didn't move. "I tried to help you, Mom, but I'm finished. I said all this before."

"I never wanted you kids to live in a women's shelter. The shame of leaving your dad would have been unbearable. Your grandparents didn't like him. I never heard the end of it."

I was silent before speaking. "You should've done what you want. You could've been happy. You still can. Your life isn't over just because Dad's out of it."

"The other man I dated ended up beating the woman he married. Your grandparents liked him. My parents blamed me when we broke up. Your dad provided a good income; he gave me you kids and he didn't hit any of us."

I stepped back out of the door frame. I folded my arms, then let them fall. My hips swayed to the left and my legs sealed together. My fists were tight and I re-folded my arms. "Dad hurt us even though he wasn't hitting us. He hurt us, especially you, Mom; finally, you can walk away from all that." I wanted to reach out to her, but I couldn't.

After a long stare, she backed away, closing the door behind her and walking down the steps to her car.

I stood motionless with the hardwood floor under my cold feet. My hands felt heavy. Closing the door, I walked over to the window and watched her climb into her minivan and drive off. I leaned against the back of the door and slid down until I was sitting on the floor. My face dropped into my hands. My head was pounding. I missed

Karl; I just wanted to be in his arms and escape from all of this.

After several minutes passed, I picked up my phone. There was a yoga class in thirty minutes. I ran up the stairs and changed, drove there and parked, not even remembering getting there or doing the class, except to hear Rebecca, a newer teacher, call out, "child's pose." I rocked my forehead back and forth seeing the memory of my mother and me arguing pour out like thick black liquid.

Rebecca's hands touched my back with a light pressure and moved down to my hips pushing me deeper in the stretch. Her breath was loud and long. I tried to breathe, my inhales short, my exhales a little longer.

In shavasana with eyes closed, I saw a vision of purple mountains by a green and grassy shoreline. I was flying in the air and so was Michelle. She looked at me with a smile and dove into the warm water. I followed and as she dove out again, so did I. The air was like the humid summers we both knew.

After the class I looked up at the window, noticing a new poster. The words, *Yoga Teacher Training in Costa Rica* were transposed over a picture showing palm trees in a blue sky and tropical flowers of orange, pink and yellow in the foreground. The yogis had sun-kissed perfect bodies.

Class ended and I stretched, wondering why no one else was on the floor. Standing up, blood rushed to my head; I saw little red dots. I bent over my knees, kneeled and slowly gathered my things, taking one last yawn before standing up slower.

"Great class, Rebecca." I caught her eye and the poster behind her.

She was covered from head to toe in tattoos.

"Thanks." She followed my gaze to the poster. "You should try it out."

"I can't."

"It will give you the peace you're seeking."

"What? I never said anything; it's probably not gluten-free. And I'm allergic to most dairy products." I bent over and picked up my block.

"It's whole grains, vegetables and fish."

"Oh." I straightened and raised my eyebrows. "I don't want to be a teacher."

"You could deepen your practice, but people who are going will be certified teachers at the end. There's space left. You're going to have to work a lot harder. It's one hundred hours of practice."

"Wow. How many classes a day is that?"

"Three. The days start at 7:00 AM and end around 10:30 PM."

I sucked in my breath. "That's a lot."

"You'll have breaks for meals and an hour here and there."

"Is that really a vacation?"

"It's fun if you like yoga. Besides, what's not to like about eighty degrees when it's the middle of winter here?"

"Are you going?"

"Yes. You could do it. Start coming to yoga more often. In fact if you don't come every day until the departure date, it might be better if you don't do it."

I looked down a moment. "Are you sure I'd be okay?"

"Probably, but as I said, you need to step up your practices. Forget about coming if you can't do that. You should be able to keep up. You'll have to teach; start learning the names of all the poses. Be present when you come to class."

I took a deep breath.

"The deadline's tomorrow. You don't have much time, especially if anyone else signs up."

"How many spaces are left?"

"Two."

"What's the resort like?"

"Go to the website. All the information is there: pictures, prices, everything. Think hard about going. It'll be tough."

"Thanks." My voice was soft and I looked away, putting my block back on the shelf and went down the stairs to go home.

An hour after looking at the website, I signed up and paid the full amount online.

-24-

Dear Eva,

How are you? My friends are looking forward to meeting you. Send me your flight details; I have a surprise.

Karl

Dear Karl,

I'm sorry I haven't been in touch. Things have been ... Well, I never told you things about my parents even though you often asked. I didn't want you to see me as flawed. But I am. My father is an alcoholic. My parents are in the middle of this horrible divorce. I hid all that from you. I saw your parents that first time on Skype and I knew I just couldn't share all this with you. I saw your happy family and I saw mine. I'm sorry. I hope you can understand.

I don't even know if I can do this long distance relationship. I tell myself lots of things how I can make it work. I watched my mom growing up; I still watch her trying to fix things with my dad. I can't be like them. I pretended none of this bad stuff was happening. I wanted you to like what you saw, someone who isn't damaged. But this is me and I can't keep pretending.

Eva

After reading the message, I logged off and reviewed the dates for the Costa Rica trip. I hadn't booked the flight yet; the days overlapped when I was supposed to be in Germany. I logged off and left for yoga practice. I walked up the steps to the studio, a minute before class started and put down my mat in the back.

Doug stood in front of the class. "Everyone, let's start in child's pose."

My forehead rested on the mat.

The pain settled in my hips. The cold I'd caught at Elizabeth's last month wasn't helping.

"Let's start in our first downward facing dog."

I remained in child's pose a little bit longer. I went through each pose until the end.

Doug announced, "Pull in your knees and give yourself a big hug. Squeeze as tight as you can and relax into shavasana."

I closed my eyes, putting an eye pillow over them. The sound of ocean waves at the beach filled the room. The volume of the tambura played on a stereo. My body felt heavy as my muscles relaxed on the floor.

I remembered the family vacation with Mom and Elizabeth in Maine when I was fourteen. It was the last time I felt peace with the three of us. Mom and Elizabeth had dropped me off at an art gallery that was giving watercolor classes in Ogunquit.

"I'm excited about these classes!"

Mom smiled. "You're welcome, Evie. We'll be back later when your class ends."

"Eva, come and prepare your palette, dear," the doting older ladies called out.

I beamed at Mom before turning back to the class.

At dinner Mom, Elizabeth and I sat at a booth overlooking the Atlantic.

"I wish Dad were here." I leaned my elbows on the table while sitting across from Mom. Elizabeth sat next to me.

We ate our fish and chips.

"He wanted to start that new job. He's taking care of us even though he's not here," Mom answered.

"At least there are no historical sites this time." I took my elbows off the table.

"I wouldn't have minded." Elizabeth picked up her sandwich.

Mom brightened. "Your dad wants the best for all of us. Even though he's not here, he loves us. He wanted to be here."

Elizabeth and I looked at each other.

"Your dad is excited about this new job. He's going to be happier."

"Mom, snap out of it." Elizabeth leaned across the table in front of Mom.

Mom looked at us. "I mean it. It's going to be fine. And the three of us girls, well, this is our time together." She reached her hands across the table taking Elizabeth's and my hands. "These are going to be our best days together. And when we go home, your dad will be with us; the drinking will stop."

Elizabeth let go of Mom's hand, but I held on.

Mom focused her gaze on me. "Want to take more watercolor classes this week?"

"Yes!"

Mom laughed. "Then give me one of your fold-over chips!"

I pushed my fish and chips plate toward her. "Take as many as you want."

Mom took one and crunched. "That was a crispy one."

"Tell us when you were in Maine before you had us."

"Before I had you girls, I was a French teacher."

"You taught French and math?" I asked.

"Math came later."

Elizabeth nudged me. "You knew that."

"Right." I sat back in the booth. "Keep talking, Mom."

"When the other teachers and I arrived at the Ogonquit shoreline, I ran on the sand and into the ocean."

"And?" Elizabeth asked.

"I wasn't in that long before I discovered its' icy cold. Out I ran!"

"Oh!" Elizabeth and I squealed like we always did.

"That ocean never gets above sixty degrees."

"That's cold." The hairs rose up on my arms.

Mom nodded with a smile.

I imagined her as a young girl in her twenties. "Did you know Dad then?"

"Yes, he was already in the Philippines. I had to save money before joining him."

"Oh." I sipped from the straw of my ginger ale. "What else did you do when you lived in Maine?"

"We crossed the border into Canada before a passport was needed."

"You were happy then, weren't you?" I asked.

Mom took Elizabeth's hand again and mine across the table. "You kids are the best part of my marriage to your dad. I love you both more than I can ever say."

She squeezed my hand, the old game we played when I was younger; I squeezed back.

I missed those days, glimpses of Mom being happy when it was just us girls. If Dad were there when we were in Maine, we'd have had another adventure, maybe more history sights but more laughs and singing, all of us together; we would be that happy family that strangers wished was theirs.

"Roll over to your side and empty out the remaining tightness." The instructor interrupted.

I held onto the memory of Mom, Elizabeth and me in Maine. I wondered how that peace, that moksha, as Michelle would have said it, would return.

At home, I logged in seeing a new message.

Dear Eva,

Now I see why you were hardly in touch. I knew there were something wrong. You're not damaged. I don't know why you'd ever think that. You should've told me before. I wish I was there with you now. I would hold you. When you visit, I'll take you to the Swiss Alps. Bring your skis. It'll be like when we first met. Let's get engaged; I know it's fast; I can take care of you like you helped me; We'll do it together.

Karl

~25~

Gwen joined my table at Espresso à Mano with her latté.

"I have something to tell you."

"What? You're finally going to the doctor?" She picked up her white mug from the plate.

"It's a cold. It'll go away."

Gwen put down her mug. "It might be more than that."

"All they're going to say is I need rest. It's a waste of time."

"You should go." Gwen placed her hands on the table.

"Can I tell my news now?"

"What?"

"I saw this poster for a yoga teacher training. I'm going. It's over Christmas in Costa Rica. I'll deepen my yoga practice for one week among all those pretty flowers and sunshine. I'll have a break from my parents' mess. I can't miss this opportunity."

"But you're sick!" Gwen scooted her chair in under the table.

"The warm air will clear up my sinuses."

"Maybe." In a quieter voice, she mumbled, "time away could help you come to your senses about Karl."

"I heard that and I'm ignoring it."

Gwen pushed back her chair.

"I'll have to wear a girdle under my yoga clothes to suck in my fat."

"You're crazy. You don't need that." Gwen inspected her coffee mug.

"You should see the people in that poster."

"Eva, stop worrying. You look great."

"If you don't take me seriously, I'll ask someone at a lingerie store. They're all sticks in there with no chest. It'll be humiliating."

"You're overreacting." Gwen shifted in her chair.

"I don't want to look like a yeti next to all those skinny yoga chicks."

Gwen laughed.

"I've hardly had time to exercise. Plus with no sex on the horizon; why bother?"

"You don't need a girdle." Gwen uncrossed her feet.

"You're just saying that because we're friends." I looked down at my bloated belly and moved the chair in further. "Where do they sell girdles? The department stores?"

"Yeah, but you don't need one."

"Do you think Target will have something there?"

"How are you going to fit a girdle under your yoga clothes? And didn't you say the room was 110 degrees? You'll sweat the girdle right off!" Gwen laughed.

"I need to buy two, times for the number of practices each day. I can't imagine we'd do more yoga than that."

"You're going to buy that many?" Gwen slapped her knee.

"That wasn't a joke. How much does a girdle cost?"

"Don't they have laundry facilities?"

"I doubt it. It's only a week."

"You should find out."

"I wish I could get a dust-buster for the belly. What do they call those things?"

"Liposuction," Gwen answered.

"Right. The girdles will probably be cheaper. Besides, what if something goes wrong with the sucking process?"

"You are crazy!" Gwen dropped her spoon clanging it in her mug.

"There's a type of massage that is supposed to take inches off your waist. It sounds too good to be true."

"That's because it is. And, you're obsessing." Gwen moved back her chair to stand up. "I need another latté."

"The girdle is the way to go." I stood up straighter.

Gwen shook her head. "After this yoga retreat, I hope you'll come back feeling more like your old self."

"I'm not planning on being a yoga teacher."

Gwen stood up. "You know deep down this is what you need. No one's devoted to yoga more than you."

"It's called survival."

After the big blowout at my house, I decided to visit Mom. Leaving her house would be easier if it came to that.

I was sitting across from her in the kitchen.

Neither of us mentioned the last time we saw each other.

"I'm going to Costa Rica for Christmas."

"What? Why? You should be with your family."

"There's a yoga retreat."

"How can you leave me? I need you here. First your father and now you."

"It's seven days."

"How do you think this makes me feel?" She stood up, opened the oven and took out the corn muffins. She slammed the oven door.

"It's too late to cancel."

"Don't these people have families?"

"It's one week, Mom. Try to be fair."

Her voice raised. "Do you want to talk about fair?!"

"I didn't tell you to upset you."

"I'm the one stuck dealing with this divorce while you go off traveling."

I flinched. "Mom!"

"Fine, Eve. Go off to Costa Rica, or wherever."

"All I want is to love you. That's all I still want. You can be happy without Dad. I'm tired of watching him walk all over you. That was the point of getting a lawyer."

Mom looked at me, a hand on her hip.

"Should I go home?"

She ignored my question. "What if you get bitten by a fire ant? They're everywhere down there!"

"I have my Epi-Pen. Besides that time was 250 bites at once. I might not really be allergic."

"Should you take the chance? If you go into shock, how will you use it?"

"I told the instructors about my allergy. I'll be fine."

"Do they have certification for first aid?"

"Of course they do," I lied, not really being sure.

"Do you know what hospital care is like in Costa Rica?"

I straightened the magazines stacked in the mail pile making sure the edges matched up.

"It's a developing country, Eve. How can you be this irresponsible? Don't you think I have enough to deal with? And it'll be Christmas."

"Mom, you're overreacting; I've spent every Christmas with our family. I need a break."

"Wait until you have kids. And don't touch my magazine pile. I have it organized a certain way."

I moved my sweaty hands to my lap, folding and refolding them together.

"You could pick up some rare virus."

"People go to Costa Rica all the time. And I haven't been bitten since that one time. I don't plan to be in any hospitals."

She turned away and banged the potato masher on the pan. She faced me. "You're not in shape to do all that exercise. You don't have the body of a twenty-year old anymore; you inherited some of my genes with this belly." Mom held her stomach with one hand. "And you've had that cold a long time. Listen to that coughing."

I looked down at my stomach and moved the chair in closer. "It's a cold."

"They'll make you get off the plane. They don't want a sick person on board."

"I'm not dying. I'll be fine."

"I've heard about people being removed from flights because they don't want people infecting everyone."

"I'm not contagious."

"You're leaving me just like your father."

I stayed rooted in my chair. It was quiet a few minutes, the only sounds were of Mom moving about in the kitchen.

"Do you want help with dinner?"

"I don't need your help," she snapped.

Some phlegm caught in my throat and I started coughing between words. "I can set the table."

"You'll get in the way. Wait until I finish cooking the meatloaf and potatoes and you've settled down with that cough."

I sighed. "I can make the frozen corn in the microwave."

"Fine."

I took out a bowl from the cabinet, poured the corn in the dish and opened the microwave. Mom stirred the mashed potatoes in the metal pot. The potato masher banged the sauce pan as excess food fell off. She cut butter from a stick, put it in and added milk, stirring fast.

The microwave hummed and I went to another cabinet getting out plates and put them on the table.

"Do you want pop, Mom?"

"No."

I took out a glass and filled it with water. The microwave beeped; I removed the corn and drained it. Mom put the potatoes in a bowl and the meatloaf on a plate and set both on the table.

We ate in silence and then I left.

~26~

December 15, 2009 at 11:02 AM
From: Bryan Jackman
Subject: Re: Time Off Request
To: Eva Weiss

Eva,

Your sales are down, not what I expect from a star rep. If you don't start bringing up your numbers, I'm going to give your top states to some of the others; your goal won't change. I'm putting you on probation. People on the team envy the flexibility I've given you over the years.

Bryan

December 15, 2009 at 11:16 AM
From: Eva Weiss
Subject: Re: Time Off Request
To: Bryan Jackman

Yes, I'm trying. I've been dealing with a lot. I need time

off around Christmas before the winter sales meeting. Vacation will help me relax and increase my sales.

Eva

December 15, 2009 at 11:29 AM
From: Bryan Jackman
Subject: Re: Time Off Request
To: Eva Weiss

I shouldn't approve this trip. Don't blow it by letting your personal problems take over. Maybe I've been too lenient with you. I'll give you this last chance. When you return, I expect 110% effort.

Bryan

December 15, 2009 at 11:36 AM
From: Eva Weiss
Subject: Re: Re: Time Off Request
To: Bryan Jackman

Yes, definitely, Bryan. Thank you for approving the time off. I will do better.

Eva

-27-

Gwen's number showed on my phone as I parked.
"Guess where I am?" I leaned back in the black
leather seat.

"Where?"

"At Ross Park Mall to buy more yoga pants for the
trip."

"Are you crazy? What about your boss? How are you
going to increase your sales?"

"You were the one who encouraged me." My voice
was flat.

"That was before your boss threatened you."

"I'll be fine."

"What if you lose your job?"

"You're the one always telling me I don't take risks."

"You should try to improve your sales."

"I can't think straight. I'm screwing up my whole life;
I've got to do something. Maybe this'll fix everything." I
was louder than I expected.

"I hope you don't regret this."

"I'll be fine."

"You say that a lot. But I know you're not."

"Karl asked me to marry him. I may as well take

vacation. What've I got to lose? I don't always tell you the good stuff. Sometimes he'd give me comfort in our quiet moments. I don't know if I can find peace on my own but I'll figure that out in Costa Rica."

"You told him no, didn't you?! Eva, have you lost your mind?!"

"I never answered him. I'll decide soon. Oh, and I told him about my parents. He was fine with it. He wished I'd just told him. See? He's a good guy."

"Isn't the yoga trip to Costa Rica the same time you were going to visit him in Germany?"

"The dates overlap. I'll figure it all out. I'd only have to ask off for a couple more days and fly to Stuttgart from San Jose. It'll be fine."

"Eva, none of this makes sense. Your job is the priority. Forget about Karl."

"I have a short window of time to shop. I'll talk to you later. Have a good one." I clicked the end button and powered down the phone.

-28-

A week before leaving for Costa Rica, I went to the doctors' hoping for a strong prescription. I had missed several yoga classes. Coughing kept me in bed. When I did make it to class, I was dizzy and ended up in child's pose sometimes falling asleep.

There was a knock at the door. Dr. Stein, a short man with graying wavy black hair entered. His kind brown eyes met mine. After some greetings, he made me stick out my tongue.

He shined the light down my throat and pressed the metal instrument inside my mouth. "Say, ahhh ..."

"Ahhh..."

He probed with the cold metal device, saying nothing.

"Ahhhhhh-" I repeated louder.

"Looks red and irritated."

"Uh-huh." I tried not to choke.

"Close your mouth now."

I moved my jaw up and down.

"How long have you been sick?"

"Six or eight weeks; it's a cold."

I should have stayed home instead of traveling to my sister's all the way across Ohio. When I arrived at

Elizabeth's, she was congested, her voice deep. Her hoarse response sounded like laryngitis. "It's a bad cold," she had shout-whispered.

"Bronchitis," he diagnosed.

I gasped.

"What?! I'm leaving Saturday for Costa Rica. I'm doing one hundred hours of yoga for a whole week."

"Consider staying home and resting." He took out his notepad from his white jacket, wrote in scribbled writing and handed it to me. "You should have come in much sooner, Eva. You always wait too long."

"I thought it would go away with rest and drinking fluids."

"Pushing yourself is not going to make you any better."

I watched him walk out the door.

~29~

I didn't think to ask about whether the Costa Rica retreat had laundry facilities for its' guests; I just thought about how much clothing I would need to hide my fat each day.

I stood in Target's dressing room line holding two black girdles. One outfit was an extra-large pair of short shorts and the other was a one piece large for sucking in the stomach and thighs.

The petite woman looked up behind the counter. "How many?"

"Two."

Her eyes gazed over the hangers and she gave me a red number two.

I walked into the dressing room and stood looking in the mirror. I took off my long dress and my brown leather boots and pulled down my stockings. Standing in front of the mirror with the bright fluorescent lights was my pasty white skin; no tan lines left. I stared back at my face and then in the mirror at the girdles on the seat behind me. I picked up the pants, extra-large first. It was narrower on the hanger than both of my thighs together. I stepped into the legs. At least my pedicure looked good. I wiggled my toes. I attempted to put my other leg in the lycra and almost lost balance catching myself on the white paneled wall. Jesus, these things are dangerous. Where's the warning label? I pulled it up and watched the magic take place. This thing could fall off if I started bouncing around; it was actually loose. I flicked the waistband hearing it snap on my skin. Ouch. I'm a large, something to celebrate. My dress dropped over it revealing my new flat tummy: not bad except the shorts were loose.

After taking off my dress, I pulled it off my body; it curled into a thick black tight wad. I unraveled it and put it back on the hanger.

Picking up the one piece for the stomach and thighs, I stepped into the first leg. This time I grabbed the wall while stepping into the other leg and then sat down almost missing the seat. Suddenly my thighs transformed into shapely pogo sticks; the girdle was comfortable. I jumped around the dressing room, tucking my fat into the spandex until I was as toned as the next twenty something. I looked at myself in my new found love: my black girdle below my purple lace bra. The red polish on my toes almost made me feel sexy.

I changed back into my stockings, leather boots and dress and walked out to the rack. I found ten size larges of the black girdle body suit and walked back to the dressing room lady.

No queue had formed. The lady looked up from behind the table.

"Excuse me. Do you have any more of these in the back?" I held them up.

"How many do you need?"

"Twenty total."

She looked at me, one of her eyebrows rising up.

"There are no laundry facilities at the yoga retreat where I'm going." I lied.

"I see. What size do you need?"

"Large. Could you get black? That nude color washes me out."

"Let me check." She put down the hangers, disappeared and then came back.

"I only have ten." She handed them to me.

"Thanks." I took the pile and walked toward the cash register. I knew of another nearby department store and would buy the remaining ones there, or, however many stores it took.

-30-

*A*fter arriving at the Costa Rican resort, I lay down on the bed and dropped my arm over my eyes dreading the first practice, the one that would show me there was no way of getting through one hundred hours of yoga. After an hour, it was time to go to the studio for the first class.

I passed an A-Frame further up the hill. A door was open. A tall red-haired man holding a yoga mat stood in the entrance heading out. He smiled and my upper lip sweat. I walked ahead on the paved trail, turning my gaze off to the right at the city far below. I drank most of my water hoping it would silence my cough. Everyone was seated; I settled on a spot near the door.

Jan and Doug, owners of the studio back home stood in front of the class in the hot and humid studio.

"Everyone start in downward facing dog," Jan announced over the chatter.

A couple people were already in the pose. Legs hopped back with both thuds and silence. Mine stepped back one at a time.

As we did our opening poses and the deep breathing began, the strength I had betrayed me.

I inhaled at the wrong time. Tension sat in my shoulders.

Rebecca walked around the studio making adjustments. "Hang your head and look through the space between your legs to the back wall."

I was looking down, then up, arching my neck even though it hurt and noticed the view outside. Out the window were the vibrant colors of trees and flowers. The lights of the city came on as dusk set in.

I looked back down and concentrated on the wall, focusing on form. I raised my head again to look out the window. My neck ached. A firm hand tilted me down, forcing me to look through the space in my knees. The hands pushed into my upper back and shoulder blades. A deep one-handed massage pressed on my neck. Rebecca stepped away.

"We'll do our first chaturanga. Come forward from high push-up to plank and hold," Jan bellowed from the front.

My shoulders burned.

"Feel your arms extend out of your arm pits. Drop to your knees as needed."

My shoulder blades pushed out, away from my sagging body; my lower back ached.

"Engage your bhandas," Jan continued. "We'll stay here for a count of five breaths."

At two breaths I'd had enough. As I looked around the room, only a couple yogis were at their knees. My breathing was labored by the fifth breath.

"Roll forward on your toes and drop down to low push-up."

I breathed in and out, unlike everyone else's deep inhales and exhales. My legs shook and crumbled. My body collapsed. As my throat tickled, I swallowed the need to cough and hydrated from my water bottle.

"Drop to your mat and turn your neck to one side." Jan called out.

We lay flat on our stomachs, heads to one side. Facing the red-haired man, I changed sides. I was hot enough from wearing all these layers, but at least the girdle thinned me out.

"Turn your neck to the opposite side. Put your hands face down halfway along the sides of your body and into cobra. Stay here for three breaths, lifting and opening your chest."

Jan's voice moved around the room and then her feet stopped, as she made adjustments, pushing tight shoulders away from ears, arching chests back into heart openers. Rebecca joined her.

"Back to downward facing dog," Jan called out from behind my row.

My knees cracked stepping back.

"Breathe in." She inhaled for an eternity. "And out. Stay here for two breaths."

My heels remained in the air unable to touch the ground, my calves screaming to be finished.

"Hop or take a step to the front of your mat and fall into forward fold. Bend your knees. Hold your elbows with opposite hands. Sway back and forth."

Crack, crack, went my knees. My hamstrings whined; I held my breath. The girdle wrapped around me like an itchy wool blanket. I picked at my shirt fanning in some air.

"Drop your heads, look down, let your neck hang. Release the tension," Jan called out.

Almost losing my balance, I dropped my hands to the floor.

"Hands on shins, flat back. Imagine your legs resting straight against a wall. Push the crown of your head forward, lengthening your spine."

Jan continued walking around the room. "Forward fold. Chaturanga."

Feet hopped back together in a jump, some landing with a thud.

"High push-up to low pushup, roll forward to upward facing dog. We'll all meet in downward dog and stay for five breaths."

I lifted my limbs backward and forward.

"We'll repeat this series a few more times with a faster flow."

I couldn't keep up and then it was too long in a pose.

My shoulder was killing me on the left side of plank.

"Take the modification." Rebecca tapped my bottom extended knee.

As we did lunging twists, I stayed firm, breathing through it and finding a spot to concentrate on.

"Pigeon pose," Jan called out. "We'll start on the left side."

From downward facing dog, my left leg was in the air until I swung it forward. My knee was so close to my torso I was almost lying on it. My hips barely moved down. Hard knotted muscle prevented me from relaxing further. My body lay flat with my forearms stretched out and the top of my head lay on the bamboo floor. My arms stretched out as my right toe pointed toward the wall. I backed off from the stretch, letting my foot lay behind me. I bent at my elbows, touched my forefinger and thumb together, the tips turning white.

Images appeared in my mind.

Mom and I sat at the kitchen table. She frowned, complaining about Dad.

My breath was loud in and out. A knot let go in my hip.

Another flash was arguing with Karl on the way to the airport.

My thumbs and forefinger pushed harder together. My jaw ached.

I looked up to see everyone else in the room motionless. I put my head back down.

I remembered gripping the phone with Michelle's mom when my parents' divorce started.

"How are you, honey?" Aunt Patsy asked.

"Okay," I lied.

Sadness lingered in my throat; it was hard to swallow in pigeon pose.

"I think of you kids often. Your parents love you and your sister. They have to work it out themselves. Tell them you love them."

"Right. I'm not talking about that. Aunt Patsy, I'm dating someone."

She sighed. "This isn't a good time for you."

"He's great. He loves the outdoors."

"You can't be dating now."

"Just because my parents can't love each other doesn't mean I can't find love."

"Yes, but— ."

My body ached. My inhale was half a second long.

I remembered telling Gwen that conversation later that week.

"That's not right." Gwen said.

The pain in my hip increased; my parents were a part of me; maybe I should give up finding peace and happiness.

I focused on seeing Michelle like other times in meditations.

"Switch legs."

I remained as the tension loosened half a millimeter.

Darren's face appeared in my mind.

-31-

We lay close in Darren's bed, our bodies warm under the white duvet. I was twenty-nine. I had bought my house three months earlier.

"It's hot." I pushed the cover away.

"Let's snuggle." He lay on his back and brought his arm behind my neck.

I smiled and moved up against him.

He leaned over, kissing me. "Hey, Beautiful. Six months. You were worth the wait."

I wrapped one arm around him from the side of his stomach to his shoulder.

Our eyes met and held.

He kissed my palm and hugged me tight; my goose-bumps rose. Tears came from my eyes.

"What's wrong?"

"Nothing."

"Did I do something?"

"No." My shoulders started shaking.

He pulled me in. "Tell me."

Tears trailed my cheeks.

He put his fingers through my hair.

"I've ruined our moment," I mumbled.

"No. Let's talk. Come on." He put on his athletic shorts and a white t-shirt. He walked out of the room to the white cabinets in the kitchen of his apartment.

I followed him while putting on my clothes.

He took out a clear glass, filling it with water. "Drink this."

I attempted to smile, taking the drink. "My tears are for your kindness."

"What?"

I looked down at my hands around the glass, unsure how to start.

He walked over to where I leaned on the counter. My one leg rested on the black stool, and the other on the floor.

"Eva, what is it?"

I didn't look up. "I have a confession."

He took both of my hands; I forced myself to look at him. He searched my eyes.

A stray tear fell. "Something happened a long time ago."

His eyes didn't move from mine. "What?"

"I tried to put my past behind me."

His warm and soft hands folded around the chill of mine.

I dropped my gaze to the wall above his shoulder.

"When I was a teenager I dated this guy; he and his family were religious. I liked how his family held hands at dinner."

"No need to tell me about old boyfriends."

"It's not that. It's about when you said I was beautiful."

He shrugged. "You are, even right now."

I looked away. "I was sixteen. Jason and I were in his room at his parents' house, watching TV. Usually the door was open because of his parents' rules. But he closed the door without making a sound and locked it."

Darren's eyes burned through me. I sat down on the stool, the back of the chair cold against my bare tight arms, my hands holding onto the seat. I stared at the green marble counter.

Darren tried to hug me. I didn't move only to feel his shoulder blocking where I had stared. "You don't have to say anything."

I looked up. "You should know what you're getting into."

He sat on the adjacent chair. "Come sit. The past doesn't matter."

I remained planted.

"I asked Jason what he was doing. I had to return my mom's car. I lied saying I had to use the bathroom. I insisted he unlock the door and went to leave. He was faster than me. He said this is what I got for being beautiful."

I put my hand out on the counter ledge and stared at it remembering his anger.

Darren stood up and put his hands on my shoulders. "You don't have to do this."

I looked up. "You need to know."

The touch of his hands felt softer. He massaged

my shoulders before moving away and sat back down. "You're cold. I'll get that blanket you like."

He stood up, took my hand and led me to the worn brown leather couch. He sat in the corner like when we watched movies together. I sat down on the edge. He brought me close into him, my back against his chest, my legs pulled in tight.

His arms rested against mine and his hand folded into my fingers. "Eva, you're freezing."

I moved to the opposite side of the couch.

Darren opened his mouth. "Eva,—"

"I have to tell you —."

He pulled a wool blanket off the floor and covered my bare feet.

I pulled the soft brown blanket up around me. "Thanks." I stared at the folds of leather on the couch. "I tried to leave. He grabbed me and pushed me to his bed. I kept telling him no. He forced me back down and telling me how girls as beautiful as me had to remember their place. I kept struggling to get away."

I looked up at Darren, his eyes sunk in, his usual smile gone.

Chills prickled my arms.

"I kept telling him I had to go. His mother tried to open the door; she banged on it. Jason's face went beet red as he pulled down his pants and took it out. I wore a skirt with dark tights that day. I struggled to roll away. He pinned me with his knee; I couldn't move. He ripped my tights and pulled my underwear down as they stretched too far over my legs. He forced his fingers inside me. I opened my mouth to scream. With the same hand that he'd dry fingered me with, he covered my mouth and threatened that if I screamed he'd hit me. He hissed names at me like slut, bitch and whore. He pushed inside me and groaned. His mother banged at the door and he moaned more. I was nothing."

"After he finished, he looked at me and told me I shouldn't have put out, that I'd failed his test. He stepped back getting off the bed. I wasn't anything anymore. I scrunched my shoulders and sat up. He said, 'now you know what it means to be beautiful.' I looked down seeing blood on the inside of my legs. I grasped my underwear down my thighs and shoved it in my purse. I couldn't meet his beaming face. I stuttered, asking him how he could do this. He laughed with a darkness in his eyes."

"I went to the door, unlocked it and ran. I remembered seeing his mother staring at my tear-stained face and then at Jason who stood in the middle of the room, his pants zipped back up and buttoned with his hand on his hips, a satisfied smile on his face. She started yelling at him. I remembered hearing, "what did you do to her," as I ran out to my mother's white Buick."

I looked up at Darren. My hands were clasped tight around my knees. He leaned over and pried my hands off my legs and held them in his. He brought me to his chest and I sobbed. He made a sound; his tears fell.

"It broke me. I wasn't human anymore." I cried.

We pulled apart, our foreheads meeting. He looked at me, his eyes red.

I looked back at Darren. "I know what you're thinking; you don't want to be with me. I'm damaged." I broke our embrace, stood up and walked away.

He reached for me. "Eva, I've never heard anything like this before."

He held me as we cried together. His hand brushed the back of my hair.

"I'm sorry this happened." He whispered in my ear.

I sobbed on his shoulder, not able to speak. My muscles ached.

"I blocked out what happened." I moved and stood away from him and stared at the floor. "It happened again with someone I knew in college. His name was Bill."

My forearm wiped my face. I cleared my throat.

All those earlier scenes that came to me that snowy day when I drove to Penn State flooded back.

"In college the group of friends I hung out with looked up to a man named Bill; he was older than the rest of us. He noticed me and we were hanging out more."

My throat was tight.

"Stop. This is hurting you." He stretched his arm, reached out and put his hand over mine.

A cold anger of shame filled my chest. "Listen to me. You need to know."

"Eva!"

I shook my head. "No."

My eyes fixated on the wall in the corner of the room.

"Eva?"

"Bill and I were studying in my dorm room but he convinced me we should go to his apartment, a fifteen minute drive through some not good areas of town. I kept trying to avoid it, but then he started calling me a prude. I struggled to fit in; I was awkward.

As we drove there, my heart raced as fear swam through me. I begged him to go back to my dorm. I lied and said I'd forgotten something. He laughed and told me what a tease I was. When we got there, panic flooded my stomach."

I stopped staring at the walls, remembering I was with Darren. I bit my lip, took a quick glance at him and looked away down to my feet.

The refrigerator hummed.

Darren reached for my hands. My gaze fixed down at the tile floor.

"I told him his back-pack was still in the car and asked how we'd study. He started to laugh. He said we weren't there for that."

I looked up at Darren.

His hands were soft around mine.

"I stood in the kitchen. Dishes piled high in the sink. It smelled of old gym socks and mold. Paper piles were everywhere. There was a table in the middle; stuff was stacked up; there was nowhere to sit. His cigarette laced kisses started near the table. He kissed me softer. I pulled away. I folded my arms and insisted he take me back. He told me to stop teasing him and grabbed my hands to the hard lump in his jeans. I wriggled out of his grasp, moved away and demanded he take me back. He told me to relax and massaged my shoulders. My tension remained. He put his hands under my shirt. I pushed his hands away and told him no. He said I led him on and insisted I put out. He pushed me toward his bedroom."

I started feeling dizzy from staring at the wall. I shifted my gaze and looked at the floor near where Darren sat.

"I tried to get away by ducking under his arms. The light was dim and a mattress was on the floor; piles of stuff were everywhere."

As the memories flooded me that snowy day when I had smelled the Patchouli at the hotel, the words poured out of me.

Snot and tears mixed down my face. I couldn't bear to look at Darren.

I took a deep breath and continued. I looked up from the floor. Tears stained Darren's face.

"I've never heard such awful things." He tried to take my hand which remained at my side.

"I left college and lived at home a semester and was forced to go to counseling. That wasn't easy either."

I breathed out; my knees pulled into my chest.

Darren stayed where he was. His face was frozen, his eyes wide.

I stared behind him feeling the space between us growing.

"After my first semester at college, I didn't want to go out alone. I couldn't do what made me feel peaceful.

If I couldn't trust my friends, I couldn't trust anyone, not even myself. I took eighteen credits' worth of community college classes."

"Why are you hard on yourself?" Darren moved toward me.

"I need to finish." My hands tightened across my knees. "One time my mom told me to stop being depressed. I told her I wanted to quit the counseling. She said I had to deal with this thing that happened. I remembered telling her to say the word, rape. I was damaged goods. Now I had that reputation she'd always warned me about. She told me to stop talking, that I was hurting her."

I looked up at Darren. "I was the one it happened to."

He dropped his shoulders. "No one knows what to say," he offered.

"She told me everyone was hurting from what happened. She said the right man would come but that I had to finish this counseling. I told her I was finished with it. She kept pushing me about it. Finally, I told her the counselor told me everything bad that happened was my parents' fault for not providing a healthy and safe home."

Darren covered his mouth.

I avoided his eyes. "My mother gasped and slapped me hard. She told me those counselors are a waste of money. I held my cheek where it stung. I stared hard at the emerald green carpet. She put her hand to her mouth, apologizing and brought me to her chest. My face was wet against her shirt. My hand remained on my cheek and my other arm at my side. She kept saying how sorry she was until I stepped back. I asked her what she told Dad. She told him and he walked past her and took a wine glass and a jug of wine and went to his office, closing the door. No one knew what to do: not Mom, not Dad, not me. I screamed at my mother to get out. I pushed her. I closed and locked the door and fell, hugging my knees into my chest. Mom banged on the door telling me to get control of myself. Things that happened after that day, I don't remember."

Darren moved next to me, wrapping his arms around me, squeezing me tight. "I'm sorry, Eva."

I held onto him, afraid this would be the last time.

I bit my lip. "After struggling for many years, a friend convinced me to see a psychologist to try to get through it. He diagnosed me with post traumatic stress disorder. He said I would always have trigger points. The psychologist said I didn't have to tell anyone what happened. It was a long time before I forgave myself for trusting those men and for what they did to me."

My palms covered my eyes.

"I thought I wouldn't have to tell anyone anymore. You said I was beautiful. I know you would never hurt me." I stopped and looked at the white walls again and stood up away from him. He walked toward me, took my elbows and wrapped my arms around his shoulders. We stood eye to eye.

"Don't leave." We stood there a long time.
"You didn't deserve this. No one does."
I couldn't let him go.

I sighed and remembered where I was, on the first leg of pigeon pose, my worse side. I stepped back to downward dog, stretching out my leg. My other leg went up and fell into pigeon on the other side.

I had loved Darren before dating Karl. I tried to date other men but what new man compared? He knew the hard parts of me that no one knew and maybe that was too much for him. No wonder he couldn't commit.

Being on my own was easier; no risks and plenty of time to focus on my career. My job had been successful until recently.

My hips hurt. All the anger flooded through me, flushing my face and tensing my hips. I wanted to cry but my eyes were dry. I gripped my hands together.

Flashes with Karl appeared: his being late for our first date together without calling. I had waited the eighty minutes for him, no matter how bad it made me feel. He'd read a poignant poem at the end of our first day meeting on cross-country skis for that meet-up north of Pittsburgh.

Deep pain pinned my hip.

I thought of my dad not showing up at my swim meets when he'd promised he'd be there.

My white knuckles clasped together above my yoga mat. Letting go, I placed my palms face down, my fingers tight pushing away the floor. My shoulders tensed, close to my ears. All of my muscles worked, my jaw tightened in fight mode.

My breathing became deeper, my fingers released and touched without pushing hard against each other. Moisture filled my eyes. Heat flushed my face. Tears fell, one following the other in rapid succession.

I popped my jaw. Deeper and longer breaths filled me as my hip dropped further to the floor.

"Release your leg, shake it out and meet in downward facing dog." Jan called out.

I wearily stretched back on all fours, quietly sniffed, wiped the small towel across my face and lifted my left leg, shaking it out. Bending my right knee toward the front, I moved my chest toward the floor, stretching out my arms, my hands lay face down like two starfish. My breathing pulsed through me. Ocean waves of breath filled the room.

"Step forward and have a seat. Prepare for shoulder stand. For those of you who are tired, put a block under your lower back and kick up your legs straight."

I grabbed my block. All the blood rushed to my head.

"Slowly come down into fish pose."

My stomach muscles weren't strong. My legs came down and my body rocked forward like a toddler coming out of an unplanned somersault.

My legs moved straight ahead on the floor, with my forearms bent behind me, my palms down and fingertips reaching forward. My chest arched in an open heart pose and my neck tilted back toward the wall. It hurt all over. My throat felt overstretched, like a tickle was about to form a cough. I swallowed hard and breathed out.

We moved into corpse pose. My muscles tingled. A warm stirring of energy moved inside me even though tightness and pain was everywhere else.

~32~

After dinner an hour later, I sat on one of several rockers on the studio's balcony. Silhouettes of shrubs with large flowers rose up near my feet on the ledge. The crickets soothed with their song. The sky was a deep blue, almost purple with a hint of red, like a sea, changing hues the deeper the water became. The city lights glowed beneath the sky. Low clouds hung like stretched out cotton balls above the base of the mountains.

Most people had returned to their rooms.

The dampness of my sweaty clothes gave me a chill.

A truck's lights headed up the hill, winding around and then disappearing into the next curve.

I looked out to the city, seeing shapes of surrounding hills and mountains. I thought of the bad memories that flooded me during pigeon pose. I stood up to go toward my room. I stopped at the massage hut that listed the different treatments and spa technicians' biographies. The reddish haired man stood with his back facing me. He turned hearing me approach. Towering over me, he met my eyes, with his, an intense blueish-gray.

Heat rose in my face.

"What's your name?" He asked.

"Eva."

He put out his hand.

"You?" I asked.

"James."

He shook my hand with a firm handshake, the way Dad taught me, showing strong character. Energy moved through me that left me flushed.

I smiled and he turned back at the board of the hut displaying massage therapist biographies.

In the light of the hut, he leaned his hand against the wall.

He stepped closer looking at the small print. "Do you know which is the blind one?"

"No." I wanted to read each one in order from left to right.

He scanned the page with his finger. "Here it is."

I turned to him. "What kind are you looking for?"

"Deep tissue or sports."

We stared at the wall.

I felt his eyes burn into me. The girdle chilled me.

I stepped away from the wall. "When did you arrive?"

"A couple days before to get used to the time difference."

"Good idea." I pursed my lips. "Have you been practicing yoga a long time?

"I had a ski accident in the Alps. After physical therapy, yoga gave me my final recovery. I've practiced since then."

"When was your accident?"

"Years ago."

I rose my eyebrows. "You're lucky."

He brushed it away.

"What do you do?" I hated asking such a bland question.

"I'm semi-retired. " James answered.

"You don't look old enough. That must be great."

He shrugged. "I'm a part-time doctor in a small village. In university, I did research that was patented. It made a lot of money. It was a fluke."

"Wow. That's impressive."

"Things happen like that. You?"

"Sales, nothing interesting. Pays for trips like these."

"You travel a lot then?"

"Yes."

"It's good you have the sales background once you have the certification."

"I like doing yoga. I did it for the peace, not to be a teacher."

He nodded. "Yoga brings a calm like nothing else."

"Yeah." My voice was soft. "It has done that." I turned away and started to cough. I unscrewed my water bottle and took several loud gulps. "I have bronchitis."

"You're sick?" James stepped back.

"Yes. It was too late to cancel. I'm not contagious."

"Brave." His forehead widened and the creases deepened.

"I didn't have a choice. I signed up last minute."

We were both quiet though neither of us moved away.

"I was going to get a cupper. Join me. It'd be good for that throat," he gestured. "And some lemon."

I shook my head. "Thanks, Doctor James. I better get ready for tomorrow." I smiled.

James laughed. "If you change your mind, I'll be over there —"

My face burned at the worst times. I shook my head. "Thanks. But no, I—." I stopped talking, crossed my arms, my goosebumps rising from the dampness of my clothes.

One of his eyebrows rose but he didn't say anything.

"Even though I'm sick, I needed the break. Well, enjoy your cupper—?"

James' eyes lingered. "Cupper — it's my evening tea."

"Right." I didn't want to be alone and think about Karl, my boss, and when the mess of my parents would end. I definitely didn't want to think about the memories I had of Bill.

"Don't look sad. You'll do one hundred hours of yoga. You'll get your certification. I'll be cheering you on." James' hands hung by his sides.

"It's not that. I'm — tired." My throat tightened. Why did his kindness make me want to cry?

"Tomorrow'll be better. Have a good sleep."

I looked up at him, still standing in front of me. I smiled and walked away.

-33-

During the next morning's practice, bright red spots dripped on my mat. Out of plank pose, my knees whacked the floor. I sat back on my ankles. The bitter taste of blood went down my throat.

Rebecca knelt down. "Eva, you okay?"

"Bloody nose." I held out my hand.

"Tissues are in the bathroom." She pointed.

"Thanks." I walked to the door out into the sunshine. My hair blew every which way. Glancing back, I caught James' smiling eyes.

Once in the bathroom, I washed my hands. Bright red liquid dripped down the white porcelain sink. I grabbed another tissue.

A knock sounded on the door.

"Come in."

Rebecca pushed it open. "Alright?"

I nodded.

"It must be the sinus pressure. Take your time." She closed the door and left.

I sat on top of the toilet lid and tested my nose. Blood dripped down my lip. I turned to the sink, cleaning up and pinched my nose once more until it stopped.

I walked back inside the yoga studio, joining everyone in crescent lunge.

Wet tissues under my fingers soaked up the stains on my mat. My knees lifted to get into downward dog. My leg stepped into crescent lunge on the left side. James caught my eyes.

After the yoga practice, I ate lunch. Warmth flushed my face as the hyena announced herself. My throat burned as I coughed and rose from the table.

"Are you okay?" Someone asked.

The hyena spoke long and loud.

Thirty-two ounces of water quelled the trumpet of my cough.

After the cough drop melted, I wandered around the resort taking pictures of flowers. James stood outside his door on the steps, his feet bare. Strands of hair fell out from his thick ponytail. He stood holding his coconut drink.

"Good?" I pointed to the round green fruit that James held.

He looked at me; his eyebrows arched down.

I looked at the hillside.

He sucked at the straw. "It's the experience more than anything. Want some?"

I shook my head. "Probably not good for the throat."

He nodded. "Nice camera."

"Thanks."

His tight curls glowed red in the sunlight.

He put his hand toward me. "Can I see it?"

"Sure."

He looked through the lens. He adjusted the zoom and pushed the silver button.

"No," I put up my hand. "I look like a rooster that put its claw in the socket."

He laughed. "You could take on anything even with this wind."

Chills rose on my skin. "Where do you come up with this stuff?" I reached out for my camera.

James faced me. "Wait a minute."

I shrugged. "Sure."

He came back with the same gray tri-pod that Karl had.

The smile drained away from my face.

We were on a trail to Mt. Democrat in Colorado on vacation together before his visa expired and he left the country. I was puffing hard as we climbed the ascent. Karl went on ahead.

"Are you ready?"

"I need a break." I grabbed onto a skinny tree on the switchback and fished out my water bottle.

"Let's go." He gestured toward the trail winding up the hill.

I unscrewed the cap of my water. "I just got up here," I puffed.

He turned around looking up the trail. "You have to keep moving to reach the summit before dark."

"You're the one who couldn't get up this morning. You drank too much last night." I gulped my water.

He glared. "I'm on vacation. I can drink as much as I want." He turned around and went ahead.

"If that was true, you'd have stopped earlier and wouldn't have passed out on the couch. And I wouldn't have had to help you get into bed." I mumbled to his back.

He wound through the pine trees, the trail becoming switchbacks. Behind me was an almost vertical drop. Seeing red and black dizzy spots, I grabbed onto a narrow aspen.

My fall would be fast and sudden, hitting trees and rocks. Putting away my water, I kept climbing with heavy breaths at every turn. Where it leveled off, Karl sat on a rock.

He had taken out his pocket knife, the hard salami, the baguette and a block of cheese. "Sit."

I sat. "The vertical drop is steep. I'm having trouble breathing."

He sliced some meat on the knife and held it out. "Here," he gestured toward my hand.

"Thanks."

He picked up the loaf. "Bread and cheese?"

"Sure."

He tore off a section of the baguette and sliced the Camembert, handing them to me on the knife. One of the slices landed in the cracked dirt and pebbles. We both looked down. I knelt and picked it up. His expression froze as our eyes locked.

"Still good. I mean, it's Colorado dirt. It can't get cleaner than that." I blew hard on the cheese, wiping away the dirt and ate it.

His smile faded. "You're right. I didn't get it together this morning." He dropped his eyes. "I want to keep going. You're alright here?"

My shoulders fell. I leaned back on the rock and set down my feet. "I'm fine here in the shade."

"I'll leave the food with you. Rest and drink. I'll be back soon." He touched my shoulder.

I looked at the sky clouding up. We were above tree line. "Be careful."

He'd already left, my words lost behind him as he hiked the narrow foot trail, surrounded by sparse brown grass and rocks. When he came back, I remained where I was, taking in the view.

"How was it?" I shaded my eyes blocking sun where he stood.

He dropped his pack and sat down. "I wished you were there." He put his arm around me; I leaned into him and he kissed my cheek.

"Eva, I was thinking." His smile left and he pursed his lips.

"Don't hurt yourself." I laughed hoping for the light in his eyes to return.

"Funny."

I braved my smile.

"I can get a university job in Karlsruhe. I've been making connections through my brother."

My heart sank. "I thought you were going to come back to the U.S. like we talked."

"No. I knew that would never work, at least not right now. I need to establish myself."

"What? But you said —"

"I know. You were upset and I had to think it through first."

"Karl!"

"Listen. I have the connection with my boss at Carnegie Mellon. We were working on a patent. My name is on it. But working with others when I'm back home at Karlsruhe will help bring collaborations together. I can have a business on the side related to the patent. And that's where you come in."

"What do you mean?"

"Quit your job and visit me on a vacation visa. When it's about to expire we can get married."

"Karl, are we ready for all that?"

"You'll be happy. You could live overseas finally."

"My career is established here."

"There's one other thing."

"What?" I slouched.

"Loan me $5,000. I'll have a side business that'll bring us added income when the patent is established. It's already in process. This could happen fast. I'll pay you back."

"Karl, that's a lot to take in. I don't know."

"We can have a future together. Just not in Pittsburgh."

I stood up, not sure what to think.

"You're a saver; you'll have plenty in your bank account."

"That's not the point."

Karl put his hands on my shoulders. "You want this. I know you do."

"Eva, where do you want to be?"

I blinked away the memory. "What?"

"I'm setting up the picture." He went across the paved trail, setting his camera in the tri-pod on the hillside.

"Right." I tried to push away thoughts of Karl.

He pushed the button on the camera and ran back. He put his arm around me.

My smile faded as I thought of the money Karl owed me.

James ran back and looked at the picture. "Eva, you looked mad in that one."

"Sorry, I was thinking about something else."

"Forget about that; we're having heaps of fun here. Yoga is about being mindful about what's happening right now. Be present with me." James looked straight ahead.

Butterflies danced in my stomach and I tried to keep them at bay.

"I'll take some of you." I stood in front of him wanting to be out of the center of attention. He went into eagle arms and chair pose.

"You're making me laugh; I can't hold the camera straight."

"I didn't say anything." He stood with his feet apart, putting his hands on his hips.

"Relax." I steadied my hands on the camera. "Ready?" I looked through the slot. "Say cheese."

"No, too American!"

"Then what?

"Queen."

"Queen like the band?"

"No, Queen Elizabeth." He looked at me, his eyes wide.

"Right. Of course." I put my hand on the button.

"QUEEEEEENNNNN!"

I took a couple pictures, then massaged my cheeks in circular motions.

"What are you doing?" James asked.

"My cheeks hurt from laughing."

"You have a beautiful smile."

My face turned crimson. "You looked great doing crow. That's my hardest pose."

"Find that focal point. Once you do that, —"

"I've heard that. I can't do head-stand because my legs are long, but then you make me look bad."

James laughed. "It's the Viking blood." He thumped his chest. "We all come from the U.K."

"That clears it up. Where's your horn helmet?"

"Witty." James spread his legs apart, his hands swung to his sides.

"The balancing poses are hardest, especially from not practicing. My muscles are tight. I wasn't ready for this. I was sick for a while before going to the doctor."

"You're getting along fine." James shifted.

I pursed my lips.

"It's the bronchitis. No one noticed aside from you and the rest of us in the back row." James winked. "Travel to Europe much?"

"Yes."

"You should go scuba diving off the coast of Egypt."

"I've never been."

"You'd like it."

"I'm a good swimmer."

"You don't have to be. All you have to do is breathe."

"Like yoga."

"Aye."

"You're peaceful."

He was quiet. "I wasn't calm in my twenties and thirties. In my forties, peace came. You have it inside, too."

"Your kindness means a lot." My throat tightened and my face flushed.

He blinked, his eyes in mine, the crows' feet crinkling as he grinned. "Ever been to Scotland?"

"No." I shoved my hands in my back pockets. "I gotta go." I gave him a smile and walked back to my room.

~34~

Doug's early afternoon vinyasa class started with the typical opening poses accompanied with fierce winds for a warm summer day.

The deep lunges while soothing to my leg muscles tensed my neck and shoulders. I struggled to bring my forearms to the mat.

The other students glided from crescent lunge to balancing half moon. Outside, flower clusters swung like pendulums; the sun remained as bright as ever.

Doug put on African drum music competing with the wind lashing at the windows.

"Follow this series with your own breath, balancing half moon to crescent lunge to dancer's pose and back to crescent lunge. Do it three times."

Though I was steady earlier, that balancing half moon made me crazy. My focal point was scattered, my breathing, heavy and shallow.

My right hand was on the block. My left palm went up with a straight arm and faced the left wall, the same as my hips to open my chest. My left leg rooted in my mat to transition into dancer's pose. My foot hit the floor, out of balance. My right leg went back behind me to start again. In the front the younger women moved like swans in a ballet.

"Breathe, people, breathe." Doug adjusted us as he walked by. "Use your breath and the flow of these poses to let go."

My eyes moved down to where the floor met the wall. Karl's face came to mind. I fell out of balance and rooted down in my standing leg, and tried to bring my other back up.

"Breathe in and out," Doug's voice like molasses reminded us.

I envisioned taking Karl's hand and walking him out the door of the yoga studio. He wouldn't move; I pushed him out and he fell away and disappeared, his eyes wide and eyebrows slanted. I left the door and came back in and took each of my parents' hands. I tugged at them in my mind.

"Release." Doug's voice brought me back.

I remained standing unable to regain my balance.

Doug announced, "Frog pose."

The mats flapped on the bamboo floor as they were turned in different directions. My teeth clenched. My face burned hot.

I looked around the room before putting a block under my forehead. My butt felt too high and my stomach sagged. I put the blue block under my stomach until it caved in around it. Then I readjusted it, moving the block sideways under my ribs. My fingers intertwined and started going white at the knuckles and red at the tips.

"Whatever you do, don't fidget."

I looked up, holding my breath, watching Doug walk around.

He put on a Grateful Dead song, reminding me of Bill from college between the Patchouli he wore and that music he loved.

The pain in my hips ached. Sweat dripped on my mat.

"I know you're hating me for this pose." Doug moved around the yoga studio.

Sweat covered me.

"You all look great. We'll be here two more minutes. You can do it. You're strong and you've come this far."

I looked up at him, two rows away.

He went along the side, disappearing from my view.

I looked down at my hands on the block and loosened them on the floor. A touch fell on my hips, pulling them toward Doug's feet, then his hands went down my back. His feet shifted to my side as he massaged my shoulders and neck.

"Let it go, Eva," he whispered.

His kindness made me want to cry. I kept breathing deep. Maybe it was only another few breaths of my life.

His touch left me and I heard the sound of disappearing steps.

Doug started talking but his words were lost in my thoughts. I heard my parents fighting and saw Mom's hurt face and Dad's glaring in the foyer. As I approached, they were silent.

Then another time: I was in my parent's kitchen as

a teenager; I picked up an index card from Dad: I'm going to the Italian club. Translation, he was going there to drink until he couldn't.

Or, the five minute calls I had with Dad asking how he was doing and not wanting to see him. Conflict washed through me.

My intuition spoke. You are more than your anger.

My muscles were killing me.

Outside the wind whipped at the glass around our studio. Several students lined the front along the windows. The wind vibrated against the tape sealing the cracks of the doors. The wind rattled and smacked the glass. The girls in front shrieked, jumping back out of their poses, the sounds of their feet moving back. I listened in horror, already imagining the tiny bits of glass thrusting forward as if in slow motion. The lush flower bushes in front of the balcony swung back and forth with violence. Trees around the studio bent over and back up again.

I remained in frog. The glass was as solid as my pose. My elbows ached on the hard floor; the mat was hot under my forearms and my sweaty palms slid forward. The girls chattered in hushed nervous voices.

"It's alright." Doug soothed. "Get back in the pose. We're almost there."

The wide-eyed young girls looked behind at us in the back row. I watched them lining themselves back into frog. My head went down, back on the two blocks, while shifting the one under my stomach to above my ribs.

The wind continued to blow its' fury with short bursts.

I flashed to Mom making me promise not to tell any-one about Dad's drinking. My hips ached as I blew out air hard and fast.

I remembered the messages written to Mom.

Dear Mom,

Karl and I are having a wonderful time hiking here in Colorado.

Love,
Eva

I had been a liar; nothing was fine.

My muscles were screaming. I'd never get out of this pose.

I remembered an argument with Mom when I saw a white index card that Dad left about going to the American Legion. Mom was in the kitchen. My eyes moved from the card to her face lined with worry.

"Why do you let him drink?"

Mom looked up. "What did you say?"

"You heard me."

I watched her eyes register. The water flowed down the sink even though there was little left to rinse.

She leaned one hand on the counter. "I don't have a choice. No one controls what he does."

"None of my friends' fathers drink like that."

"You don't know that."

"My friends' parents drink on special occasions like Easter or Christmas. For Dad it has to be more."

"I don't know where this is going but you better stop."

"Or what?!"

"If it wasn't for me, we wouldn't be a family."

"Right, because we have to pretend that we're a good one."

"Your attitude needs to stop."

"My friends' parents love each other. You and Dad hardly hold hands."

She paused. "Your dad isn't affectionate."

"Why do you let him?" I wanted to nail her this time.

"Eve, you don't understand anything."

"Then make me."

"There's no stopping him."

"Why can't you try?"

"He's head of this house. I can't question him. I can't make him do anything. Where do you think we'd be without your dad?"

"Happier?"

"No. We'd be poor. I can't raise you two without your dad's income."

"But Nana and Pop could take us in."

"No."

"But why?"

"I told you. We have to stand by your father. Like it or not, he'll drink when he wants. I can't stop him. And it's not always bad."

"People get divorced when they're not happy and you aren't."

"You want me to break up this family?"

"It isn't right that we have to grow up pretending it's fine when it's not. Why do you make us do that?"

"Because social services would come. They'd tear up our family. We have to stay together, even if it's you girls and me against him."

"But you're not happy."

Mom shut off the water. She looked down.

"Why can't you be the head of the household? You do everything anyway."

"Because it isn't done that way. My role is to listen to your father and do what he says."

"Mom, it's not the 1950s."

"Your father already tells me I'm never good enough, no matter what I do."

"You run things as it is."

She didn't look up.

I pushed out the anger with my breaths.

Another memory flashed. My parents' voices were raised. They were standing in the living room near Dad's blue leather reading chair.

"Your money doesn't do anything for this family." Dad yelled.

"You're unemployed and you're not helping. All you do is stare at that TV. I work hard, make dinner, clean the house and help the girls with their homework."

"That's women's work."

"You could help them with their science assignments."

"I tried but all they do is get upset."

"You can't yell at them when they don't know the answer."

"If they want to get anywhere in life, they have to work harder. You coddle them."

"You should never have had children."

"That's your job," Dad answered with a sneer. "Now, leave me alone."

Dad walked down the steps to his den and slammed the door. Mom's steps pounded into the kitchen.

Vomit came forward in my mouth; I swallowed hard with my belly forward in frog.

I remembered Karl and I had decided to go to the park one morning. I sat in my car, waiting for Karl to get ready; we were supposed to leave thirty minutes ago. I called his phone; it rang a number of times.

"What?"

"Karl, where are you? If you don't get in this car in less than three minutes, I'm leaving."

"In a minute." He hung up.

He emerged from my house and opened the car door.

"If you hadn't been drinking so much last night you would have woken up on time."

"You're over the top. My boss is on my back and now you are."

"Get out."

"Oh, come on." He tried to reach for my neck.

"We're late meeting Gwen because of you. I told you to get up an hour ago. And I did let you sleep it off."

Karl tightened his fists by his sides.

"I'm sorry, babe. I have a lot going on." He reached for me.

"Get off me. I'm driving. And don't call me, babe." I put the car in drive and pushed the pedal hard. "Did you remember to throw the wash in the laundry?"

"That's your job."

I stopped the car and the brakes lurched us forward.

"What did you say?"

"I was just kidding."

The throw up came back in my mouth. My breathing was shallow. I swallowed the vomit back again as the memories continued playing in my mind. I blew out a long painful breath. I stretched my fingers long on the floor. My stomach was in knots, the sour taste lingered in my mouth.

We were on one of our regularly scheduled Skype calls.

"What do you mean, you spent all the money I loaned you?"

Karl shrugged. "It takes a lot to start a business."

"When are you going to pay me back? Did you ever think about that while you were spending my hard-earned money?"

His face was blank. He looked away from me.

"I can't believe you." My face burned and I got so mad I pushed the red button to end the call. I wanted to hit something.

"Twenty more breaths. Make them count." Doug's voice brought me back.

My stomach made a noise. It felt heavy, thick like lava.

"Let me hear your breaths."

My stomach churned and the sour taste rushed up, faster than before. I rolled over, my body stiff from the pose. I ran from the room, opened the sliding glass door and rushed out, holding my mouth. With one hand on the brick wall beneath the windows, my body heaved and I threw up. My hair blew all over in the wind.

I stepped away from the mess. I sobbed, looking at the pale green and yellow chunks covering the bushes.

The glass door slid open.

"Eva?" Rebecca approached.

I turned my head. Vomit came up again in my throat. I didn't wipe away my tears.

"Don't worry about it. We can hose it down. Here's a towel."

I took it. "I'm such a mess."

"Are you dizzy?"

"A little."

"Go back to your room and lie down. Come back and join us when you're ready."

I saw kindness in her eyes.

I tried to smile, but tears came instead.

"Take care of yourself. I'll prepare your mat and things for when you return."

I nodded and walked away on the path, headed to my room.

Opening the door and walking to the bathroom, I brushed my teeth. I splashed my face with warm water and lathered face cleanser, feeling the cool soothing beads. Salty tears disappeared with water and soap. I stared in the mirror. My eyes were red and puffy. Tears fell again. I sat on the toilet, my hands covering my face. I paused looking back at my reflection. I'm not fine. I never was.

I sobbed and didn't look away from the mirror. The hurt fell away drop after drop. I stood a while, shifting my feet, leaning forward on the sink, watching the sadness melt down my face and chin. The drops went down my neck. I turned on the shower and took off my sweaty clothes. The water was hot, steam rising up. The water pressure drilled into the top of my head; gurgles went down the drain.

I took in a deep breath, having forgotten what expanding my chest and lungs was like. I stood in the shower, counting ten breaths in, ten breaths out. The shower stopped and I reached for the towel and looked down at the drain, imagining all that hurt, all those patterns of my parents in me, all that heaviness, washing down, hearing it swirl away.

The white robe comforted me, the soft waffle pattern warm against my skin. My hair was tight in a towel turban.

I walked toward my bed, stopping to look at the hillside and the orange flowers outside my balcony. I draped across the bed, loosened the towel around my hair and closed my eyes on the softness of the pillow under the white bedspread. The sun warmed my ankle.

The slats on my window were open with sounds of birds chirping and wind blowing through the leaves and stalks of flowers. I fell asleep, stretched, rolled over and opened my eyes, looking at the clock. Forty-five minutes had passed.

A memory flashed: I was seven and sat on a walnut chair from the kitchen table that faced the oven. Mom was cleaning the kitchen standing at the sink facing the backyard.

I squirmed in my chair. "They're not moving."

Her back was turned as she washed dishes.

"What, honey?"

"They're not growing," I pointed to the muffins baking.

She turned before she bent in front of the oven. "Oh, look! One grew higher."

"Where?"

"The one in the back." She pointed.

I looked intently at the oven, holding onto my blanket that went with me everywhere. I put my thumb in my mouth.

I stood up from the chair and wrapped myself around her leg.

"Honey, you can't do that. I need to get dinner ready. Sit in front of the oven door. Keep watching. One of these days you'll catch it. I've seen it many times. Watch real close."

I sat back on the chair and stared at muffins that never moved while she bustled around the kitchen.

Her gentle hand brushed the bangs off my eyes as she moved past me. She held her hand out and I took it. She squeezed three times and I did it back, the game we sometimes played. She smiled and let go.

I pined for that closeness with my mother.

I stood up from the bed and walked back to the mirror.

My eyes darted around and then back at me. I stood there until my feet hurt.

I walked back to my bed and slept on top of the cover. The wind whistled through the open slat of the windows. A chill rose on my skin. I rolled over and stretched, stood up and changed into yoga clothes to return for the evening class. It was late now.

There was a knock at the door as I was about to leave.

I opened the door partway.

James stood with his hands by his sides. A small smile appeared and the creases in his eyes deepened. "How are you?"

"Okay." I remained in the doorway, my ears burning.

"I can listen."

I bit my lower lip. "I'm fine. Thanks. Not now."

He paused, looking at me with searching eyes.

My smile faded. "I need to get ready, James. I'll see you later." I closed the door, not sure what I was feeling.

A couple hours later, the practice before dinner had ended.

I put my hand on my hips and then walked to leave the studio.

The others rolled up their mats and started heading toward the door.

"Hold up a minute," Doug called out. "We have one question before you all go."

As we moved our mats to the back, we formed a circle.

Doug settled in among us. "I want you each to answer the question: 'Am I angry or blaming someone?'"

When it came to my turn, my lips were pursed. I licked my lips. "My dad is an alcoholic. I have covered for him since I was a teenager. My mom made me promise not to tell anyone or social services would separate us." My voice shook and I took a breath. "I feel guilty telling you all this, but I can't deal with keeping secrets anymore." I put my head in my hands and wiped away shameful tears.

James reached over and put his hand on my shoulder as I sat cross-legged. I let his kindness kiss me.

I continued, "I am angry and blaming someone for letting me think all that pretending was normal. And I'm furious with my guilt but it's what I know." I put my knees in my chest, bowed my chin and squeezed my arms around my legs, pushing James' grace and anyone else's far away like the wall of protection that had grown inside me all these years.

The room was silent for a full minute. I stared at the clock, away from everyone's pitying faces. I wondered when I could get out of here. Someone else spoke, but I didn't hear. More people shared and I heard bits and pieces while staring away from the group.

I heard James' voice and caught his face, meeting his eyes.

"I've let go the anger from when I was younger. The blame stopped years ago. After my mother died of cancer, my father hit the bottle a lot. It was just my brother and me. I had to take care of him; no one took care of me. We all missed her."

James broke our gaze.

Others took their turns.

Everyone stood up.

James walked over to me. "You were brave sharing that."

"So were you."

"I spoke up because of what you shared. I remember what it was like." He put his arm around me. "You may not believe it, but you're brave."

I let him be close and broke away, making excuses about needing to get to my room.

~35~

At dinner, everyone was inside avoiding the wind. Two women my age sat together. They turned, looking up at me.

"May I sit here?" I touched the chair.

"Have a seat," said the strawberry-blond with the ponytail.

I put my hand over my open mouth. I drew in a quick breath.

"Eva?" The blond one said.

I shook my head and blinked. I stepped forward and leaned on the table. "I — uh ... I'm dizzy." I lied.

The freckled woman brushed her strawberry hair behind her ears. She looked up at me. "You look pale. Sit." She pushed an empty chair out across from her.

"Right. You just—"

"What?"

"You look like someone I — Maybe I should go. It's been a hard day." I didn't move.

The woman's eyes creased the way Michelle's did. "Join us. You trusted our group to share your experiences. That took courage and strength."

Tears brimmed my eyes and I blinked hard.

"Thanks." My voice was quiet. I set my plate and glass down, sat and put a white napkin on my lap.

The woman's coloring was fair. She was as curvy as Michelle before the cancer.

I looked up, shaking away memories. In the books I read about loss, one author wrote it was normal to see resemblances of the lost person. These moments faded like grief.

"Remind me your names?" I let the thoughts disappear.

"I'm Julia, and this is Liz," Julia, her long blond hair pulled back in a pony tail gestured toward Liz, who looked over at me with Michelle's eyes.

"Eva, what you said was brave." Liz drank her water.

"What do you mean?"

"About your father."

My face flushed. "I feel guilty even though no one knows him." My voice shook.

Across the table, Liz and Julia leaned in.

Julia jumped in. "I had an uncle who drank a lot. I'll bet almost everyone in the room has a heavy drinker in their family."

I remained bolted in my chair unsure what to say.

Liz leaned in. "What happened to your uncle?"

"He drank to death."

I covered my mouth and sucked in my breath. I sat back. "I'm sorry."

"Alcoholism is a selfish disease. Only the drinker controls it."

"It's easy to feel like I'm the only one who understands what it's like having a parent who —."

"No one talks about it." Julia placed her hand on the table.

After dinner we were back in the studio.

"Listen up." Jan shouted over the conversations in the room.

The chatter stopped. "Start counting off by twos."

I pulled my knees into my chest. I was a one.

"Twos on this side." She pointed to the windows facing San José.

The crowd scattered.

"Ones in the back of the room."

I looked to the door wishing to escape without anyone seeing. Doug passed us blindfolds. I draped it around my neck, tying it once from behind and lifted it to my eyes and then into a knot. Once Doug checked that no one could see, I heard footsteps from the others moving toward us.

"Everyone form a line with your partners and follow Jan."

Sweat formed above my lip.

My partner's pressure was soft but firm across my back. I felt rigid and wanted to escape. I shifted my feet feeling unbalanced. My breath went short and fast.

My guide intertwined her arm through mine and her balance shifted to me. She moved a small step forward, but I didn't go. My arm moved but the rest of me stood still. I could hear the others stepping and felt the air as others walked around us. I told myself I was being ridiculous. It's just a silly game. No one's going to hurt me.

She stood for a moment where she was ahead of me and then back-tracked to me putting her arm around my shoulders starting to move forward. Heat ran through me. Were it not for the tightness of the bandana, tears would have fallen. A stranger was being kind; that was all. I moved forward with baby steps as she did. Others laughed as I tried to take longer breaths. I felt the first set of the steps under my toe pads and froze. Again, my partner let me feel my fear, went back up the step where I was. She moved down and waited, not moving again until I did. We walked down a step and the hand pressed on my forearm. I took a step, one foot at a time until I felt the unevenness of the grass. Sounds of movement of others came behind and ahead of us.

Humid air greeted my skin. Evening birds chirped. Sounds of pots and pans banged above in the cafeteria. My partner moved to one side and I turned and stepped into the grass where the fire ants slept. We padded through the grass, back to the paved walkway, up the steps and back into the studio, a little faster than the way down.

My guide surprised me with a hug and patted my hand. Softness fluttered in my chest. I swallowed hard.

"Thank you, Eva." The woman's voice said.

I smiled, not trusting myself to speak.

"Ones and twos go back to your sides." Jan called out.

There were sounds of feet shuffling, talking and laughing.

"Remove your bandannas," Jan shouted over the noise.

I took mine off and looked at the people across the way. I wiped away the tears at the corners of my eyes, and turned to look out at the night sky. My heart lifted as I took in a deep breath. I'm safe here.

It was almost 10:00. I turned toward the door to leave.

"Listen up. We have one more."

My tired eyes met a woman's across the room. Deep lines of wrinkles sat ingrained around her eyes and mouth. She was on both of my flights from Pittsburgh.

Doug shushed us. "Form a circle."

There was a buzz of conversation as we waited for our next instruction. I stood next to that woman.

"Count off by fours." Doug's eyes moved around the room.

When the counting finished, Doug divided us into four groups of seven.

We all spread out. I made eye contact with Julia, Liz and James, as we moved away from each other. I was with a group of the younger women.

We were given tiny white slips of paper. Frog. My heart sank.

"Fours, don't share what's on your paper," Jan announced.

She and Doug handed each of us fours a blindfold and tied it behind us.

"Animals, go find your herd!" Doug yelled out.

"Hissssss ... Meow ... Ruff Ruff ... Ribbit ... ROOOARRR ... Oink ... Quack Quack."

I smiled then laughed, listening for ribbits.

"Ribbit!"

I turned toward a frog sound. Muted meows and barks wandered to the other side of the room. One of the ribbiters held onto my arm leading me across the floor.

"Ribbit," a deep voice followed as I felt a hairy arm through mine.

"Ruff Ruff, Hiss, Meow," I heard farther away.

"Ribbit, Ribbit, Ribbit..."

New voices took my hands and my other arm.

Jan's voice was loud. "Fours, take off your bandanas."

Liz, James and a couple others stood in my herd as we shared one of those belly ache laughs.

~36~

I walked toward the door after a long day.

"Eva," James called out.

I turned.

"Wait up." He remained, waiting for others to pass before approaching. "Have a minute?"

"Sure." I searched his eyes.

"Join me on the chairs outside the studio. The wind's died down." His hand rested on the small of my back.

Goosebumps rose on my arms.

"Cold?"

"No."

We sat in the corner of the balcony away from the glass doors. He turned one of the chairs facing me. I looked out at the valley.

He looked to the horizon and returned his gaze to me.

I gathered my hands in my lap and settled with resting them on the chair. My sandals fell from my feet while stretching them up on the banister. Bright orange painted toes shined in the darkness.

We looked ahead at the night sky.

"You were gone a while today."

"Yes, I was resting. You didn't have to stop by."

"I had to."

I looked at him trying to read his thoughts.

He was quiet a minute. "What you said tonight took courage."

I pressed my tongue hard against my teeth. "I don't see it like that."

"I know."

I stared out at the canopy of trees below.

"Look! Did you see that?" He pointed off to the right.

"What?"

"A shooting star."

"Did you make that up?" I laughed, surprised by my rising anger.

James knitted his eyebrows together, frowned and clasped his arms across his broad chest. "No. Keep your eyes open."

I turned to him. Sweat rose on my upper lip. "I'm sorry. I don't know why I said that." I stared at the sky. "I should tell you —"

"There's one." He signaled. His other hand moved covering mine.

I bit my lip before answering. "I see it." I glanced at the side of his face and then back at the sky. I knew I should tell him about Karl but with his hand covering mine, his kindness was hard to let go.

"Eva —"

"James —"

We spoke at the same time.

"Go ahead." I blinked and smiled, regret heavy in my stomach.

He smiled at our exchange before his face straightened. "Your eyes are sad. I want to help."

I shook my head. "It's complicated. I'm sorry. Or, it's not. I need to go." I took my hand away and stood up.

He rose. "Stay. We could sit here together not say anything, and keep watching the stars."

"I can't. I mean, thanks. I can see you're a good person. I have nothing you want to hear."

"Eva, you're upset."

I forced a yawn. "No, I'm not. I have to go." My words came out fast.

"I'll walk with you."

"No." My throat tightened. "I'm hardly sleeping; I should be relaxed here." My voice rose, higher than I meant. My fists clenched at my sides. I stared hard trying to keep my watery eyes from spilling.

"What's wrong? Did I do something?"

"No. Nothing. You're kind. I'm just — exhausted." I stood in front of him, stalling. I took a deep breath. "I'm fine." I looked at him and forced a smile. Tightness rose in my chest. I stepped back and his hand dropped away. I would just not tell him about Karl or anything else.

"I'll walk you back."

I shook my head and faked another yawn, covering my mouth. "I'll see you tomorrow."

I glanced at his wide eyes as I started taking big steps.

"Good night, Evie." He called behind me.

I stopped and turned. I was at the opposite corner of the balcony. "Only my dad calls me that."

"I meant to say Eva."

"I haven't seen my dad as much because, my parents, they — " I shook my head. "Never mind. See you tomorrow."

"Aye. If I did anything I hope you'll tell me."

"Really, it's not that. I'm sorry. I need to go." I turned.

Sweet dreams, love." His words followed me.

-37-

The wind started up again and blew hard much of the night.

I tossed and turned a while, picked up a book whose page I kept re-reading. The wind whistled through the slats of the windows as it broke through the trees. Getting back in bed, re-adjusting the foam pillow, I pulled up a cool sheet and quilt over me. I thought of James' hand on the small of my back. My heart sank as I thought about Karl.

I got out of bed, rolled out my mat and did a couple vinyasas. I went to the bathroom, noticing dark circles under my eyes. After 2:30 AM, I went to bed having a dreamless sleep.

When I woke, the curtain billowed out like a big balloon.

My left obliques ached. I rolled onto my stomach and then my side, facing the view.

My knees went up to my chest. Sharp pain in my abs caused me to gasp.

A bird chirped in the distance and then another squawked.

The threatening dark clouds moved away, scattering

quickly to the left. It was getting brighter out, the dawn disappearing into daylight.

I remembered James telling me that my eyes looked sad.

I tried to imagine telling him about being raped, about Karl and about all of it, and if he would ever talk to me again. I shook my head to clear it.

During the morning walk, we followed dirt paths as wide as logging roads similar to the ones Dad led hikes on in Forbes State Forest. A rainbow far in the distance covered the sky over lush greenery of the coffee plants.

This quiet walk was unlike the hikes Dad led; he would sing a song and a couple people would join. The summers were green like here, lush with ferns and thick green woods, mossy rocks, slippery from the morning dew.

I looked ahead, away from the memory of Dad and back to my walk on the dirt roads. Guilt filled me knowing I had outed Dad about his drinking.

I caught up to the group when they stopped at an overlook. From the left were thick green tree tops mixed in with rusted tiled roofs in the valley. To the far right, the city sat far below with all different colored buildings looking like a Cézanne painting.

I felt eyes on me. I turned my head and James caught my glance.

I watched him approach and tried to feel neutral.

The others stood further out on the cliff.

"Did you sleep well?"

"Sorry about last night. I was overtired. I don't know what came over me."

"No need. Your strength shines through. I like being with you." He touched my forearm.

I nodded, smiled up at him. I bit my lip asking myself what I was doing. "Me, too."

We continued to walk, silent in each other's company, sometimes his arm brushing mine. The walk stopped at the cliff's edge, trees and shrubs bordering the gate where it dropped off.

Looking at the border I remembered the steep jagged descent from a climb in the Rocky Mountains with Karl.

I recalled a fight before leaving the hotel that day. I slammed the door on my way out away from Karl's gaping mouth as I grabbed my lime pack.

The trail's dry dirt crunched under my boots. Many people hiked in front and behind me. My brown fishing hat blocked the already bright late morning sun. A man my age and his dog walked past. I smiled; we exchanged hellos.

I took big steps. Karl and I were a nightmare. My parents were an even bigger mess.

There were fewer people as the trail became as narrow as footsteps. The hotel and much of the mountain town had fallen from view. Behind me jagged snow covered mountains filled the horizon with a bright blue sky behind it. To my left was a green lake with a pathway over the dam. Below, a lone mountain biker crossed the middle. Farther ahead to the right, steep rock faces fell with crumbled rocks toward the bottom. To the distant left above the water was the jagged mountain, barren ground above tree-line. A carpet of pine tree tops lay beneath the snow base. I continued hiking without Karl, wishing Dad was there, like the days before the divorce.

I looked up to cross the street back to the yoga resort after the quiet walk had ended.

James stayed with me all that time on the walk. Guilt clung to me about Karl.

~38~

After lunch I arrived for my deep tissue massage with José. His beady eyes were cross-eyed and sunk in his sun-drenched face. I wondered if he'd been blind all his life or if it came later. Black hair was shaved close to his head. Lanky and tall, he stood in the doorway. After some greetings, he led me into the room. A cream sheet covered the black table thick with padding. White curtains hung along the wall.

"Place your clothes on the chair." He put his hand on the back of it.

"Thanks."

"I'll wait outside and knock before entering. Lie under the sheet face down."

I undressed, piling my clothing on a chair. My face fell down in the neck rest; I stared at the stringy cream rug and pulled up the white flannel sheet to cover my chilled skin.

José knocked on the door. "Ready?"

"Yes."

The door opened, the knob clicking. Then it closed, hitting the doorframe.

"Are you warm enough?"

"No."

The sound of the cabinet door opened; the weight of a blanket draped across me. He moved it, uncovering my back. Cold air bristled my skin. My arms folded along my side. My hands tightened in a fist; goosebumps rose. His touch was light, his frigid fingers moved down my back, around the rotator cuff.

"Relax," José whispered.

My breaths remained short as I tried to lengthen them. My exhales became a little longer but my jaw stayed tight.

He stopped, lifting his fingers from my skin and pressed the muscles of my hips. The crunchy muscle moved away under his hand.

José pressed the point of my hip, soft, then deeper.

I gasped, my reaction when my parents bad-mouthed one another.

José's voice was barely above a whisper. "Let it go."

I mumbled into the headrest.

"What?"

"I don't know how." I said, my congestion building.

"Release the muscle."

I breathed in and out. The tightness remained. "How?"

"Breathe into the pain."

My fingers curled at my sides. My mouth opened releasing my teeth. I saw my mother's scowl followed by Karl's. My jaw was as braced as before. I moved my head further down as I remembered running to my car that first day visiting Dad's house. Silent tears fell.

Thoughts of Karl weighed heavily in my stomach as I remembered when we were on Skype. Karl sat at the dining room table in his parents' house.

His parents were home and we had a chance to meet online.

We exchanged greetings.

His dad, a tall man with white hair spoke first. He leaned down behind Karl sitting at the table. "Eva, what's your job?"

His mother was on the other side of his dad peering down at the computer.

"Eva is the best salesperson in her whole company." Karl announced.

I raised my eyebrows. "I've just been here a while. I've only been the top salesperson one year out of ten." My voice drifted off.

He interrupted. "You're my number one."

I breathed out as José's fingers worked down my calf muscles.

His hands moved down crunchy lower back muscles. I stiffened.

"Relax," his soft voice commanded.

I struggled to breathe. The knots in my neck remained.

Guilt seeped inside me like a dark shadow. I remembered Mom upset about my leaving after telling her I'd be in Costa Rica.

Though my eyes were lightly closed, I blinked them multiple times feeling moisture wetting my temples. I blew out wondering if my muscles felt any different.

"Good."

His fingers landed on my left hip, the worst pain in all of my body.

"Breathe."

I tried, four long yoga breaths.

"Good. Inhale as deeply as you can. When you breathe out, I'll put pressure on your back. Exhale as long as you can; push out everything."

I breathed in. As I exhaled, he pushed hard, cracking my back. Stress had held dark thick pain as multiple cracks sounded. Relief swam through my body like quick new energy.

José lifted the white sheet at an angle. Chills formed on my skin as I flipped over. He replaced the warm sheet and blanket. Under my head, he pushed pressure points with his fingers. Lifting my head and turning it to the right, he stretched my neck muscles. He moved my head to the center and turned it to the left. His fingertips rested under my head for a minute. Intense pressure sliced from my shoulders to my neck like a cutting knife. I held my breath and bit down. Moving his hands away, he stepped to the opposite end; his feet shuffled on the floor. Some pain fell away like a dark shadow. He uncovered the blanket, pulling my feet. The left one made a hollow popping sound.

He pushed on my quads and I gasped, wiggling away from the tickling spasm.

"Relax." He lifted his hands and tried again.

I stayed still holding my breath.

"Good start," he answered. His hands moved over

the covers and my exposed arms, one at a time. His touch drifted over my forehead. "Eva, I hope you liked it."

My eyes remained closed. "Thank you," I whispered.

"You can stay here as long as you like. I'll be outside."

I lay on the table listening to the sound of my breath into whatever opened spaces existed. A tear fell out of the corner of my eye.

There was an afternoon yoga session but I didn't rush trying to get there. Instead I sat on the chair on my balcony looking straight ahead thinking of how the massage made me feel. It took all my energy to move, get dressed and be among others.

The small group training was in progress as I walked through the open glass door. Each group had four students doing a series of the same poses while the other led.

Rebecca looked to the door without smiling. "Eva, go to James' group." She pointed to the opposite back corner.

"You look relaxed," said Brad, the college graduate.

"I was lying down for an hour and a half." I snapped.

David, looking to be in his fifties with his graying hair and high forehead looked at me. "You alright?" He stood over me.

I shrugged. "My muscles are tight. I couldn't relax."

"Which massage therapist?" James asked.

"José."

"Did you like it?" David asked.

He turned and I noticed the diamond stud in his ear.

"I don't know." I stopped looking at the others and stared at the clusters of flowers growing in front of the balcony.

Everyone stopped asking questions, but in my peripheral, I watched their faces with widened eyes, shaking their heads.

"José was fine; I couldn't relax and that's my fault." I studied the floor.

"Someone else lead in your group." Rebecca announced.

Brad led us through a small segment starting at downward facing dog. David and James went after him.

Rebecca approached my group. "Eva."

My faced burned; sweat formed on my upper lip. "I'm not going to be a teacher."

"Eva, please."

"I'm not like everyone else."

"You can do it."

I turned away from her. The three men in my group greeted me with smiles.

"I was late for class. I might not remember the order of all the poses that you taught in the beginning."

"You knew what time class started." She crossed her arms.

"The timing of my massage went over."

"If you were serious about deepening your yoga practice, you'd have showed up on time. You're here to do the work just like everyone else in this room."

I looked at her, not blinking. Heat rose in my face. I breathed in deeply and exhaled.

Her voice softened. "Teach this practice. I know you have it in you." Rebecca reached to touch me.

I moved away from her and blinked hard, tension building in my shoulders. I stared at the wall behind the students in my practice class. "Start in plank pose." My voice felt like icy steel.

They squinted at me, any trace of smiles disappearing. I didn't dare look at James.

"Breathe in and out." I wasn't even starting in the right pose. My shallow breathing returned.

"Down to halfway-push-up and hold."

I gave them two seconds.

"Upward dog," I commanded like a drill sergeant.

They shifted their weights forward, arching their backs.

"Downward facing dog."

They looked at me, waiting for the next cue.

Rebecca stood tapping her foot, then shifted her hip and tapped with the other; she crossed her arms.

I blinked hard.

Brad moved his right foot forward.

"Yeah, do that one. I can't think of the name. Shit. What's it called?" I put my hand in front of my lips trying to remember.

The others mirrored Brad going into a lunging and balancing pose.

"Yes, watch Brad. D-D-Do what he's doing. I'm sorry I don't know all the poses. I'm tired."

"Crescent lunge pose." Rebecca corrected. "Eva, you've got to remember the names of these poses. I told you to prepare before this retreat and you didn't show up daily as I'd advised."

"Right." I looked down and put my hand on my forehead. "Uh... Crescent lunge pose. Take a few breaths here. Twist to the right putting your elbow on your knee." I was confused which leg to show them. "Breathe here a moment or two. Good. Step back to downward facing dog and shake out your legs."

I caught Brad's expression. His sunken eyes narrowed and the red splotches on his face matched his hair. In downward dog, he let out a loud and fast sigh.

I listened to their longer breaths, while trying to do the same.

"In out, in out, yes, that's right," as if hyperventilation was the way. "Do the other side. Umm, opposite whatever was before." I studied which foot was forward. "Now your left."

Feet changed positions.

"Sorry, I meant your right."

And their feet moved again.

"Moon lunge. Hold onto that stretch."

They looked up.

"You look good." I turned my glance to James.

His eyes brightened.

I took it as encouragement.

Rebecca repeated, "Crescent lunge pose, Eva. Did you even look at that booklet of poses I gave you?"

My face burned. Sweat formed above my lip. Tears waited behind my eyes. I tried not to breathe. "Right. Crescent lunge pose."

"Twist to the other side. Ummm..." I tried to think which was their right and left.

"Put your elbow on the other side."

Jan's voice interrupted the groups. "Change."

Everyone stood up.

Brad looked right at me and mumbled, "Practice a lot if you're ever going to teach."

"I didn't come here for that." I barked at him, louder than planned.

James moved next to me. Out of the corner of my eye, I saw him rise taller, clench his fists at his sides, take a step closer to Brad, and gave him a stone-faced stare.

People from other groups looked in our direction. Desperate anger hovered inside me. My teaching covered me like a heavy blanket of shame.

-39-

After dinner while drinking tea, I sat next to David and Suzy. My eyes dropped away as I stared out at the coffee plantation. They gabbed about their families, jobs and the latest new restaurants.

My mind drifted back to the Green Mango, thinking about Dad, wondering if one day it would be comfortable between us.

I watched David and Suzy talk.

"I do my workouts on the weekends when my son's mom has him. I have him during the week," David continued.

"How long have you been separated?" I asked.

"Divorced."

"Sorry."

"It should've happened a long time ago."

"Why did you wait?" I picked up my mug.

"For my kid."

"What?"

"To spare him."

"Kids know more than you think." My face grew hot.

"It wasn't easy," David answered. "My wife dragged it out."

I sighed. "My parents are divorcing. They can't stand each other and they think my sister and I want to hear it."

"Divorce isn't easy for anyone." David sat back in his chair.

I clasped my hands on the table and rested my chin into my hands. My eyes closed and my throat tightened.

The conversation stopped.

David's quieter voice started again. "No one talks about what drinking does to the people they love. I see it in my practice a lot."

"Covering for my dad hurts."

David looked straight at me. "You're not alone, Eva."

"I hate keeping secrets. I wish my parents had divorced years ago. I wish they could've been happy."

"Why'd they wait?" David asked.

I gasped. "They liked their dysfunction?"

Suzy and David exchanged glances and retreated back in their chairs.

"They stayed together for the kids," my voice rose and shook at the end.

Suzy leaned forward, her eyes softening.

"You ever been married?" David asked.

"No."

"I wondered if my marriage was worth it. I look at my kid and I know it was. Your parents feel the same; trust me."

"Maybe." I looked at David's ring finger. It was evident where the ring had been.

I remembered once sitting on my parents' bed while Mom curled her hair.

"Why doesn't Dad wear his ring?"

"He lost it years ago." Mom stared at me in the mirror. I didn't look away until she did.

I was quiet sitting between Suzy and David as they talked.

"Are you ready, Eva?" Suzy asked.

"For what?"

"We're heading to the studio for the evening practice," she continued.

I looked at them both, standing up. They watched me. I met their eyes. "The massage wore me out."

"It does that," David said.

"Right."

They walked in front of me. I followed down the steps, listening to their chatter.

During the evening practice, we went from downward dog to standing poses, proud warriors I and II and back down to chaturanga. We hovered in forearm plank. My knees collapsed. Sweat dripped. My hands clasped together, fingers in a death grip.

"Turn your head to the left and stretch out your neck. Line your arms along your sides, palms facing up," Jan called out.

My clothes stuck to my skin, moist with the fat sucker suit underneath. We were in locust pose.

"Turn your head to the right," Jan continued.

"Shavasana."

I imagined the sludge weighing me down dripping out of my skin like tar through a black grate.

"Take a ten minute break. Next, we'll practice assisting."

After the break, we gathered in the room.

Jan spoke. "Pair up."

Her voice was loud over the talking of others. "Assisting gives a deeper stretch and can improve form. Practice it and give your partner feedback. Start in mountain pose."

I turned my head, meeting James' gaze. He signaled me to come to his mat.

"We'll practice the same movements." Jan continued.

"I'll go first." I stood up, my face flushing wishing it would stop. "I mean assist."

He winked.

"Mountain pose." I watched his shoulders move down his long torso.

"Breathe three times in and out." I listened to his deep ujaii breathing. "Forward fold."

His body fell over. My feet stepped closer to his. Sweat formed on the top of my lip; heat surged in my arm pits. My hands pressed up the sides of his back and down his shoulder blades. With my right hand, I massaged the base of his freckled neck and tilted his head. His steady and deep breathing calmed me.

"Breathe at your own pace for five breaths."

My fingers worked a longer massage on his neck.

"Table top and chaturanga."

He jumped back to high push-up, his feet landing in silence. His toes moved forward to low-push up and his chest arched up. He went back to downward facing dog.

He stood, facing me. "Brilliant."

"Thanks. My pressure?"

"Super."

"Good. Your turn."

He called off the poses; my body fell forward. Goosebumps formed as he touched my skin, his breath close. The heat of his palms moved over my back. His firm push on my head released my overextension and his fingers moved down with a quick neck massage.

He called through the rest of the poses after hanging in forward fold. We rushed through the last poses.

Jan's voice interrupted. "Time to wrap up."

I went to downward facing dog and stepped forward, stood up and turned to James.

"Thanks. You were great." My eyes rested in his and this time I pushed away my guilt.

The creases under his eyes broadened and the lines deepened around his temples.

I went back to my mat.

"I'd like to hear some comments," Jan spoke above the chatter.

Many hands rose. Jan picked one.

"I liked having the deeper stretch."

"Yes," Jan nodded. "Someone else."

"I was in their personal space and it felt strange."

Everyone laughed.

"Who else?"

I raised my hand halfway.

Jan met my gaze. "Eva."

"It was like learning a gift." My face burned.

She nodded and called on a few others.

We had a fifteen minute break before the group meeting.

Jan spoke, "Listen up, everyone."

Our large group silenced to a whisper, conversations coming to a close. "Everyone get in a circle."

All twenty-seven of us formed one.

Doug waited until everyone had paper and pen. "Write down an answer to this question: What is the worst thing that could happen to you?"

I wrote:

That I will die alone.

"Now fold up your piece of paper; Doug is going to collect it." Jan held up the hat.

I stared at my paper, folded it multiple times and clenched it before pushing it toward the bottom of the pile.

The hat ended up in Doug's hands.

"Doug will walk around; pick one of the pieces of paper," Jan instructed.

My face sweat.

"When you pick one, read it aloud and empathize. Respond with your advice in how to overcome it."

I crossed and re-crossed my legs.

When it was my turn, I read the response:

"The worst thing that could happen is to be a failure and let others down."

I paused, letting these words sink in before responding.

"It's easy to feel like that. Focus on the positives by writing down triumphs for the day."

When I looked up at everyone, Jan nodded. "Are you practicing that now?"

I shook my head. "Not in a long time. But it had helped."

As people read answers, I was surprised how many had an answer similar to mine. I leaned in. Advice included spending time with friends. Or, doing favorite activities to meet people and make new friends.

As the exercise finished and the conversation became loud, Jan's voice rose above everyone else's. "One more exercise."

I sat back down hugging my knees.

"You have fifteen minutes to meet three people and find out why they came here. Go."

A woman stood next to me.

"I'm Cynthia."

"I'm Eva."

"I'm here for vacation. My commitment is to feel the joy in every day," she told me.

I smiled. "I'm here to reward myself for a hard sales year." I took a deep breath and the truth came out: "That's not it. My commitment is to let in the light and be open to love. What I want is a deep connection with a man and to know our loyalty, love and respect for each other is mutual."

Cynthia came forward and hugged me. "He's out there, Eva, waiting. Believe it."

My face burned and my throat got tight; I nodded in her light embrace, and breathed deeply fighting the tears that arose inside me. Telling that desire was frightening. Michelle had been independent and happy and didn't need a relationship except at the end, before —. Mom and Dad were together but what kind of love was that? Did marriage even work? I wanted to believe that man was out there.

I met Monica next and then Laura.

James met my gaze. I blinked and lost him in the crowd.

I was back in my room, getting ready for bed. I thought back to the massage and berated myself for holding onto pain.

It was after midnight. Sleep wasn't going to come. I got up, dressed, threw on jeans and a t-shirt, looked in the mirror, and put on lip gloss. My eyes adjusted to the darkness. I turned on the flashlight and walked up the path. The lights in James' A-Frame were off. All across the resort was silent. I walked back and sat on the corner of my bed. I picked up my laptop to go to the pool area where there was wireless access. The water lapped against the blue mosaic tiled walls and the crickets chirped. The night sky glittered with stars.

I opened Skype and put in my ear buds. Karl's status showed he was on. I pushed the green phone button. It rang several times.

"Karl? Are you there?" I typed.

I waited.

He typed. "Eva? I wasn't sure I'd hear from you."

"Can we talk?" I wrote.

"Yes," he typed back.

I pushed the green phone line button and he answered. The video appeared on my screen. His hair was disheveled and his eyes were puffy.

"How are you?" I asked.

"Awake."

"What were you doing?"

"Lying in bed about to get up."

"I needed to ask you — "

"I'm spending the Christmas holidays alone. Why would you go to Costa Rica to be around a bunch of strangers?"

"Were you serious about getting engaged?"

His voice was quiet. "Yes."

"I think about my parents and then about us."

Karl was silent, his lips tightening.

I tilted the laptop screen and looked past it at the trees and listened to the crickets.

"Eva —"

My arm pits felt sweaty. A chill ran over my arms.

"What did you want to say?" I looked back down at the screen and watched him shift.

He said nothing, so I blurted out: "I can't end up like my parents."

"We're not them." His eyes softened.

"I see similarities and it frightens me. I've repeated their patterns."

He shook his head. "It'll be good when you visit. We'll find other dates for you to come. I get that you had to do this yoga thing."

"Karl, you're asking me to give up everything."

He pursed his lips. He sat up straighter in front of the pillow. The skin that doubled his chin disappeared.

"It isn't going to work. You drink like my dad and I can't deal with that." I put my hands on the table and pushed away in my chair.

"Eva, it's not a big deal. You're getting nutty with all that yoga drivel."

Heat flushed me. My voice raised. "You know nothing about what yoga does for me. You never listened; you never took the time to understand. And, I do know what it's like living with an alcoholic. I've already covered for you."

"What are you talking about?"

"It doesn't matter. It's the fact that I did it."

"Look, I know your parents' divorce is tough. I have problems, too. And being away from you isn't easy. But these comments about my drinking are ridiculous. You're reaching."

"How dare you."

"You didn't have to go on that yoga retreat. You chose that over me."

My voice was loud against the lapping of the pool. "This isn't going to work. You need to send the money you owe me." My joints ached from making fists.

"Eva, come on; you're overreacting."

"You're an alcoholic."

Darkness crossed his face. "You're crazy."

"I will not do it again. I lived it with my parents and I won't choose that in my relationship with you. I will not have it."

He opened his mouth to talk. "You already did."

"Don't say another word. We're finished. Send the money I lent you."

His lips pressed in a tight thin line, his eyes wide.

As he was about to speak, I hit the red hang up button. I stared at the light in the pool illuminating the empty lawn chairs. My heart raced. I closed the laptop screen and took deep breaths. I stretched out my fingers and sat back in the chair. The moon glowed. The night sky was bright and beautiful. I stared at it, my thoughts racing from my father to Karl. Despite the memories, the deep breathing calmed me.

Feeling something crawling on my arm, I shook it and moved my head to the side, my neck stiff with sleep. As the moon had moved higher, doubt fell away like darkness.

-40-

The birds chirped and another day of sunshine greeted me from my room. I had slept past the morning walk and breakfast. On the fourth morning of practice, sweat poured from me. After class I walked to the balcony of the studio. Others had gone to lunch.

James sat looking out at the views of tree tops below.

I put my hand on the top of his chair.

He looked up and smiled. "I was waiting for you."

I sat next to him and leaned back.

"Sleep well last night?" He asked.

"For once, yes." I looked away from him watching the sky above the green hills.

"Something on your mind?"

"No."

My mind wandered to Karl and the call last night.

"I need to talk to you."

"What is it?" I pulled my legs in, hugging my knees. A shiver ran through me.

"When I was fourteen, I was studying less, focusing on football and being a kid. Our football is your soccer."

"I know."

"My parents pushed me toward medical school

because of my teachers' encouragement when I was fifteen. My mum and dad worked hard to make sure my brother and I would be well-educated. Not long after, my mother was diagnosed with breast cancer. I thought it was my punishment. My dad told me to be an example for my little brother while Dad took care of her. She suffered seven years, getting better, only to get worse."

James' face fell as he talked, the bright and cheery glint in his eyes gone.

"I went to university; I didn't want to leave my mum, but she insisted. It was my year of exams when she died. Dad was lost without her. He worked long hours at his firm. When he was home, he was hitting the bottle. I carried that shame of her death for years; I regretted not helping; I'll never get that time back."

I dropped my feet to the ground and turned facing him. "You did the best you could."

His hands lay loosely on the armchair. "Yes. I learned that eventually."

He looked away and stared at the sky before talking again. "When my shame wasn't there, anger replaced it. I worked long hours to avoid letting anyone get close. Years later when I had my own practice, I bumped into an old teacher from school; she said I had my mother's eyes. She said things about her I never knew."

I looked in his eyes. "You are peaceful."

He smiled and reached for my hand, smoothing his fingers over them. "I choose to live this way; happiness is a choice. Even when my family became lost as my mum got sicker, she never stopped fighting. She kept going. That's how you are. I felt that connection the first day we met."

I shook my head. "It isn't the same thing. I'm not fighting death."

James' voice rose. "You have strength. I see you fighting hard. My mum did the same. I haven't seen another woman carry it like you. You're a survivor. I know this, Eva. Trust me." His voice softened after he said my name.

He was as soothing as the sun on my skin, the sound of the birds twittering, the beauty of the brilliant colors of the flowers all around the resort. He was all the calm that Michelle had ever given me.

My goosebumps rose despite the warm air. "James, I don't know what to say. I'm touched. I — "

"You're safe here. No one's going to hurt you." He squeezed my hand.

I dared to look at his face.

He turned his body to me.

My eyes shifted, staring at the tree tops, hearing the birds, seeing the calming blue sky once more. We sat there a while, not speaking. I didn't notice the time passing.

"Thanks for sharing that, James." I bit my lips. Congestion grew inside me. I tried to stifle a tear from falling. I didn't move to brush it away or speak to explain. I blinked and let go. The birds sung and my face relaxed. I could almost smile.

He looked at me a long time, a gentle turning up of his lips.

James made no gesture to move and we were quiet.

"You're helping me." My voice wavered. Tension fell from my neck as I sat back in my chair watching the clouds.

"I see your sadness. You're carrying it around like I did. Whatever it is, it's not your fault. You're a fighter like my mum. She never voiced it; she lived it."

I looked away from him, past his shoulder, seeing the sun near my A-Frame.

"We all hurt, but we don't have to keep it."

I turned back at him, his eyes soft, as he leaned toward me.

"I'm sorry you went through that."

He nodded. "I think of her each day. I got through the grief, not over it; you just get through the hard bits in time; the memories flooding in, the picnics by the sea, the bedtime stories, the football matches. One day peace returned."

"There are a lot of things to say. I wouldn't know where to begin." Fury burned in my chest. I clenched the sides of the chair.

"Tell me when you're ready."

"Losing your mom must've been hard."

"I had a second chance to change. As do you. No matter what happened, you can find happiness and peace. It's in your heart."

He stood. He opened his arms for a hug.

I turned my head feeling his chest rise up against mine. My chin almost rested on his shoulder. His arms were firm around me. James' forearms wrapped behind my neck against my hair, his hands on my shoulders. I wanted to cry. My chest burned, that familiar tightness. My body melted into him. His arms wrapped around the middle of my back. Tears fell as I tried to breathe normally. We stood like that, not shifting. Sobs gave way. He held me tighter. I breathed deeper giving in to him.

After a while, he stepped away, and loosened his arms. He held my chin in his hands. "Give me that smile."

I looked up at him, not trusting my voice.

"You'll be right as rain, I promise." His eyes bore into mine until I looked away.

At lunch I sat on the porch in view of the coffee plantation.

Suzy approached my table. "May I join you?"

"Sure. Look at those two little birds on the wire. I wonder if they're dating."

She laughed and sat down, setting down her glass and plate full of food.

"How are you doing with the practices?" I asked.

"Good. Better than expected."

"You must work out all the time."

"Thanks, but some of that is genetics." She glanced at her arms.

"I don't look like the typical yogi."

"You're worrying too much, Eva."

"I travel a lot for work. At first I tried to work out at

the hotels, but there is always work. I used to be thin like you."

"You're beautiful."

"I need to drop some pounds. The girls here look like the gymnast I was never going to be. I can't even do a cartwheel or a handstand. I look around and everyone's doing it but me."

"This is your yoga journey. You've been places no one else has been. You've had struggles others haven't. You have strength."

My elbow was on the table, holding up my chin. "Do you believe that?"

"Yes."

I sat back in my chair, my hands on the armrest. "What's your yoga journey?"

Suzy put down her utensils. "Teach yoga. Schedule time to volunteer." She picked up her mug.

I listened. "What else?" I asked.

"I don't know."

"Does everyone always know the answers?" I looked down at my plate, the food mostly finished.

She shrugged, looked down and scooped up a bite of quinoa and mango. "You must be getting better. Your appetite is coming back; you cough less."

"Yes."

"Do you want to have children?"

"No." I pushed an onion off to the side with my knife. "I don't want to pass alcoholism on to a future generation."

She put down her fork and knife and looked at me.

"You wouldn't know it to meet my dad. I hated how he chose it over us." I moved the onion under the un-eaten lettuce.

Suzie's eyes widened and her cheeks stretched tight, the wrinkles, faint lines on her face.

I moved my hands to my lap. "I see a therapist."

"That's good."

"He's encouraged my yoga and meditation. He's helped me in ways no one else could."

"Self-awareness helps."

I looked up.

"You have strength in ways some people can't reach. Did you ever think about telling your dad how his drinking affects you? I did once."

"Did it change anything?"

"Not for him. But it did for me. I was standing up to what wasn't right."

"I tried. He denied it. I don't know that it made much of a difference."

"You should tell your father what it did to you and your family."

"I did. He shut down the conversation."

"You could write a letter. You wouldn't have to send it if you didn't want to."

"My mother suggested a letter once when my cousin died. It didn't bring her back. Time passing helped. I still miss her. But thanks anyway."

"I'm sorry about your cousin, Eva. Look in the mirror and see your respect. It's in there; trust me."

I picked up my tea as the hot liquid soothed my throat. I set it down. "Thanks." My voice was soft.

"Writing the letter will help you let go of that pain. Your dad needs to hear what it did to you. It needs to sink in with him. It could change things."

"Did you do that with your father?"

"I wrote him a letter after he died. He was violent when he drank. Living was easier after that."

"Wow. I'm sorry you had to deal with that. Sometimes my dad's words hurt." I looked at her.

"It was a long time ago, Eva. Addiction is abuse. None of it is good. Letting go that pain helped me live a happier life."

"Hmm."

We both lifted our mugs and drank our respective tea and coffee.

Her lips curled. "James was talking about you."

My face burned. "Oh?"

"When he spoke your name, his eyes lit up, sort of the way you're blushing all of a sudden."

"I feel connected to him; I know I shouldn't. The timing is all wrong. It started as soon as we met. I feel like I've known him a long time. I can't shake that feeling."

She nodded.

"He told me something that mattered this morning."

"I saw you two holding hands."

I thought of him while looking past Suzy's eyes.

"Live in the moment. Get to know him. It's clear he wants to be around you."

"The thing is, I'm engaged. Or, I was — until last night."

Suzy's forehead rose.

"It's just — I can't talk about it. I have to go."

Suzy shook her head.

"Everything's complicated; it's not how it should be." I stood up and left to get ready for my watsu aquatic body treatment.

Across the path from the massage treatment hut, the watsu area was a hot tub shaded by a big square umbrella. To the left was a pine cabinet of fluffy white towels and plastic chairs. A waffle bathrobe sat folded on one of them. Another cabinet was on the right.

Mateo greeted me with his soft brown eyes. He stood lean like a cyclist in blue swim trunks. He shook my hand. A light shadow of a dark beard was on his tanned face. His shorts were the same color as the umbrella top.

The water bubbled. Tiny ceramic square tiles lined the inside of the tub.

I stood on the concrete above the steps into the water. The valley of palm trees and banana trees, shrubs of red, orange and pink flowers, stood before me. San José was hidden by the lush tree tops and green hills.

"A pleasure to meet you, Eva."

"Thank you." A rush of warmth filled me.

"I put a robe on the chair for after the treatment."

He gestured. "Get in, and, I'll be there in a minute."

"Okay."

I stepped down into the water, feeling the soothing splashes against my skin. The water came up to my belly. It cascaded over my shoulders as I bent down. I tilted back my head and wet my hair.

Mateo put a clipboard into the cabinet on the right and set a pen on the counter of the shelf. He walked into the hot tub.

"I'm going to hold you from your head to your feet while you're floating. I'll hold you up the whole time. Your body will move around in the water. Let me do the work."

I nodded.

"Later on, I'll put you underwater. Do you need nose plugs?"

I shook my head.

"I'll tap you on your shoulder like this."

"Okay."

"Ready?"

"Yes."

"Start floating on your back. I'll support you." His eyes met mine.

I raised my feet to the top of the water, trying not to splash. My head fell back, my ears in the water. My eyes closed.

The side of my arm touched his toned chest. "Sorry."

He paused. "I'm going to chant. It'll be the sound of one letter. While I do that, take deep breaths. Set a silent intention of what you want this treatment to represent."

I breathed in, hearing the sound of the water thinking of what it would be like to have peace inside me.

His fingers were under my head and his other hand rested lightly on my lower back. When my ears came out, wind blew the shrubs' leaves against each other. Chilled air hit my skin. I shivered, dipping the exposed parts back in.

"Mmm...." He chanted.

His voice muted and vibrated as my ears floated in and out of the water.

Slowly he turned and my legs moved to the right. I floated the other way, back and forth, like a slow pendulum. Energy flowed in my body. He moved me to the side; I felt his chest against my back, the cloth of his swim trunks behind me.

One of his legs was up and around to encircle me. One hand held my head, while the other moved down pressure points of the sides of my neck and shoulders, down the arms, then the hips.

I was floating on my back. As my ear came out of the water, his deep voice filled my mind.

"Mmm...."

The swirling started again. The hot water moved around and over me; his fingers worked down the other side of my arms, legs, neck, back and shoulders.

I saw myself as a little girl on a swing set going higher each time touching the blue sky with my thin white socks in my patent leather buckled shoes under my dress. My blond hair reached past my shoulders. It was like watching a silent film.

Then I became an adult, an ice skater twirling round and round, faster and faster in Rockefeller Center. Next I was a young girl running around in a circle, Michelle and I reaching out to each other, our hands pulling tight as we giggled. The summer breeze flowed around us. We both had on our Sunday best dresses. The sun warmed our bare arms. Then the little girls were gone.

I saw blue sky and pink and white dogwood flowers reaching above a trestle. Then it was me, laughing as an adult, all the beauty of nature above me.

Mateo turned me on my side and pushed my knees into my chest. At first I resisted. He held his arms around me. With his hands, he encouraged me to wrap my arms around my knees to keep them there. He hugged me as I floated in the fetal position. Sadness drifted away.

These moments repeated, the swirling around back and forth and then the pressure points on the opposite side. I savored the heat of the water, the sounds both in and out, the waves lapsing on my body, his touch, and the energy of the bubbles as they moved around.

Two taps fell on my shoulder. He pushed me under when I was on my back. I held onto his arms and didn't let go. I opened my eyes in the water; panic filled me as I scrambled to come up for air.

He hoisted me up. "Are you okay?" He looked down with kind eyes.

I nodded unsure where my fear had originated.

He waited and my grip loosened. My head and shoulders leaned toward one of his arms that stretched across my back. He stood still, holding me like a husband about to cross the threshold with his new bride. My head and shoulders fell so that I was on my back, even while he cradled me.

"Take long breaths. Inhaling..." His chest rose against my side. "And out."

His obliques went down with my own exhale. My breathing became a longer breath, deeper than the last few months. We stayed like this a while.

I breathed out, pushing away fear, pausing at the bottom, feeling the emptiness in the pit of my stomach. I took a long inhale.

His fingers tapped my shoulder and I held my breath. His hands pushed me under water. My body twisted around, going deeper. I imagined what swimming in a deep blue sea among fish and marine life would be like.

He wrapped my upper leg around his back and shoulder and with one hand, he massaged from my neck to my fingers. It was like taking a big sigh under water. He massaged both sides of me and flipped me over while keeping me close. He let me float on my back and held the nape of my neck with one hand and then let go.

I was floating, relaxed enough to sleep. The water moved around me, from my shoulders down to my feet. Something soft was under my foot; brain tissue like in biology class, bright colors: blue, green and yellow filled my mind. The spongey feel cushioned my feet. I breathed in and out, the exhale down to the pit of my stomach.

Opening my eyes, I discovered that softness was his pruny fingers. My toes were being pulled forward and out. The water moved beneath my feet. A current of water lapsed beneath me toward my head. His fingers landed in pressure points on my temples.

"Thank you, Eva." He let go and stepped away.

The movement of water swirled, the shift of his warmth gone.

I stood up wishing to remain floating.

"How did you like it?"

"Amazing."

"Do you have a close sister?"

I looked at him, raising my forehead. "A close cousin."

"I sensed something about a sister."

"My cousin died not long ago. She was like a sister."

He looked at me, his eyes light and soft. "I'm sorry." He paused. "Your bathrobe is on the chair."

"Thank you." I walked out of the water and into the fluffy white robe.

That evening after yoga practice, we formed a circle to do an exercise.

"Count off by ones, twos, and threes," Jan shouted over the hum of conversation.

"Ones, line yourselves up across the front of the room and face us."

I sat there, glad not to be a one.

"Twos," Jan shouted. "Choose a one and face them, nose to nose. We want to see little space between you. You should be toe to toe, eye to eye and no talking."

As the twos lined up, I wondered what was in store for us threes. The ones and twos looked awkward, standing close, as if trying to arch their backs and shoulders away.

The closeness between the ones and twos lasted a few minutes.

"Twos, change your positions so that you're facing out. Ones, you're finished. Go sit down. Threes, get up there and face the twos, toe to toe, eye to eye in silence."

I walked up there.

James stood; I caught his eye and he smiled. His eyes were red, ready for sleep. I faced him. If I lost my balance, my lips would land on his chest. His exhales landed on my cheeks.

I looked up in his eyes as if we were sharing a secret. I wanted to wrap my arms around him like this morning. My heart was pounding, wrapped in our space together.

Interrupting my thoughts, Jan spoke up again. "Twos and threes, you're finished."

James and I remained standing close as the others dispersed.

"We should go," I whispered and stepped away, holding onto his forearms for balance. He gave me an amused half-smile.

I walked back to sit where my notebook was.

"Write down two or three lines about this experience," Jan called over the growing chatter.

A few moments of silence followed as we wrote.

"Who wants to share?"

I raised my hand.

"Eva."

"It was intimate, almost better than a kiss." Heat flushed me.

There was a hush around me.

"Nice," Jan answered.

"Who else?"

"It cracked me up." One of the twenty-somethings spoke.

"It made me wish I'd had spearmint gum," someone else answered.

I looked at the girl who'd said it and laughed along with the others. I listened to more answers and turned my head, looking at the group behind me. James caught my eye and winked. I grinned back.

His lips moved. "Lovely."

-41-

As soon as my head hit the pillow, Suzy's suggestion about writing Dad entered my mind. The clock read 11:24 PM.

Dear Dad,

I'm finished keeping your drinking a secret. My relationships with men are horrible because I've grown up watching how you treat Mom. I can't believe I thought that was normal. Wake up, Dad. It isn't the 1950s. Women become scientists and engineers or whatever. They choose to get married or not. Your sneering comments about Elizabeth, Mom and me hurt; we're your family. How dare you treat us like we're lesser than you.

I told Mom to get a lawyer who would fight for her. I couldn't take watching you walk all over her once more, dictating what she can and can't have.

The father I needed was the one who could admit to his alcoholism. You could've admitted it when we were at the Green Mango, or any other time. But, no; you deny it. Mom would've helped you. We would've gotten through it.

Other people take risks; I can't. I feel like a

disappointment because I haven't followed in Elizabeth's footsteps of having a family. When I take risks or decide to make a change, I feel so guilty, I can barely stand it. Growing up it was depressing being told I could only be a teacher, nurse or librarian, because, according to you, those are the only career choices for women. You ruined my dreams about art. Art schools wanted me, but you told me I would never be good enough.

Having a family is a trap. I see what it's done to Mom. I have the right to choose my own life.

Do you really think I wanted to come to your new house the way you treated us?

I'm not covering for you anymore. I'm sick of being hurt. I don't know when I want to be in touch again.

Eva

The tears were already streaming down my face. I looked at the written words that were engraved inside me. I thought about having covered for Karl in front of Gwen. I sobbed and threw my journal across the room, smacking it against the wall. Hot red anger surged through me. I wanted to do something, make it burn, make it hurt. But I wouldn't do that; I couldn't; I'd had enough of that. I put on my exercise clothes and sneakers. The door slammed; humidity greeted my skin. I ran on the path outside my door with big jolting steps of what it is to not be a runner. I pushed out the pain with every screaming movement. Every time my foot landed on the pavement felt like throwing a glass, one after the other, the sudden crash of my body pounding the earth. I ran under the balcony of the yoga studio toward the small cabins and around those paths. Some lights were on. Loud crickets soothed me. I kept running in circles because that was all I had. I returned to the room, tired and sweaty. I took a long shower, rinsing everything I felt down the drain.

During the night after having slept some, I pushed away the covers and opened the balcony door. The air was calm, the birds quiet. I felt numbness and sadness of all that had stayed inside, and, maybe empowerment. What would happen if I did send that letter?

~42~

The morning sky was a blanket of grayish-blue clouds with hints of pink. The dense mass rested above the mountains like intimate friends.

I stood up out of bed, my muscles stiff and aching with each movement. I picked up my journal from the floor and opened it. I re-read the lines of the letter, lost my balance and reached for the bed. Lining up my journal above some magazines on the corner of the coffee table, I walked out to the balcony. I came back to the stack and put a magazine on top of my journal.

I thought about waking up in the middle of the night, to send the letter or not. I felt everything at once: anger for carrying the secret all this time, sadness and guilt for telling a room of strangers about his drinking.

As the sun came up, I remembered it was our "See Costa Rica" Day." We had three choices: a tropical jungle hike highlighting waterfalls, a volcano tour or a ride on a zip line. I'd never seen a volcano before and thought of the pictures to share with Dad, but now that I wrote that letter, who knows what our relationship would be.

Estefan was our guide. Handsome with his brown skin, his deep voice had a soft accent on the ends of his words, like dark sultry chocolate.

As we drove along, Estefan explained the personality of the rains, the healthcare and education offered to all Costa Ricans.

As he continued, we wound our way to the edge of the volcano. Watching the scenery pass, I was comforted seeing ferns growing along the road.

I thought of hikes with Dad like that one foggy morning when it felt like we were walking in a painting. The mid-July ferns lined the trail with old growth hemlocks mixed in with blooming rhododendron and mountain laurel.

When we returned to the resort, I was tired from the day of touring. Those from the zip line group looked elated.

Evening settled in as I sat outside on the rocking chairs on the studio's balcony. The soft wind blew like a backdrop behind the chirping crickets. The stars sparkled. Cracking floorboards were to the left. Someone was stepping closer, joining me in the darkness like that first evening.

"Eva?"

"James."

He laughed. "Aye."

"How was the zip line?"

"Brilliant. I wished you were with me. What did you see, the volcano or the waterfalls?"

"The volcano, but there was a cloud over it. Seeing the ferns along the trail made me happy."

"Other people had a fear of heights but they did it. We were all there for each other."

"The day reminded me of hikes with my dad."

"You and your father are close?"

"It's complicated."

"It often is." He smiled and paused. "Tell me."

"I have trouble letting go."

James touched my hand, intertwining his fingers over mine. "We all do."

The wind blew on my skin; a chill ran up my spine. The instructors were in the studio, their energized voices muted through the glass. We sat away from the window.

"I don't know where to start."

"It doesn't have to be in order."

I didn't answer and looked out at the sky, easier than James' eyes.

"Say what makes you comfortable."

I turned back to him.

He sat back in the chair, his feet planted on the ground.

I sat in the adjacent chair. "It's like my parents have been separated for years living in the same house, but now that they're getting divorced, it's stirred up everything. I tried to be neutral, but helping one means hurting the other. Yes, my dad drank and and none of that has been easy. He's still my dad and I am close to him. I wish I could've made him stop. Dad gave me his love of hiking. Often it's just us or with other hikers in the Sierra Club. What's hard is all the years of pretending it was fine when it wasn't."

He tilted his head and leaned toward me.

My knuckles cracked and I moved to stand.

"Stay." He leaned forward.

I paused, conflicted. I licked my lips and put my fingers to my temple.

"Don't go." His warm hand touched my arm with a gentle pressure.

I put both of my forearms on the armrests and fell back down into the chair, bending one knee. My sinuses started blocking up.

A bird squawked in the distance.

I took a deep breath. "When I was a teenager my mom made me promise to keep Dad's drinking a secret. No one outside my family knew about it for years until I told my therapist; I felt guilty about that and cried hard. It was horrible telling it during the group exercise. I feel ashamed for talking about it but I won't take it back."

"We want our parents to protect us. Sometimes they can't. We can't prevent them from hurting themselves. You can't control his addiction."

I remained silent.

"You're aware of what keeping secrets did to you."

"Yes." My voice cracked.

"You're strong."

"I didn't ask for any of this."

"Nobody does."

"I don't know why you still talk to me, especially what I said about my dad during that exercise." My voice went to a whisper. Heat rose inside me. My throat burned. I turned away and studied the planks on the deck by my feet.

He pressed my forearm.

I turned to face him.

"When I lost my mum, and all that happened after, it wasn't easy. We all have struggles and we all want the same things: love, respect, and to belong. You're not alone. Your strength shows in being here right now."

I wanted to run but turned and looked up at the sky. "I used to talk to my favorite cousin, Michelle, about my dad's drinking. I could trust her." I paused.

He moved his fingers slipping through mine.

I continued. "She died of cancer; I miss her." My voice broke.

I blinked away tears.

"I'm sorry about your cousin." He paused. "Your parents made you keep abuse a secret. They might not be capable of showing what a healthy relationship is."

"Abuse." I mumbled. I knew he was right but it felt wrong hearing it aloud. I wanted to defend my parents. "They did the best they could."

He nodded. "Most parents do."

My hand was lifeless inside his. Goosebumps grew as my hand became clammy.

"You're cold."

"I'm alright." Chills rose on my arms and I pulled away tucking my chin into my knees.

"Take my pullover."

"I'm not cold. Talking about this hurts."

He covered my knees. "Goosebumps are rising on your skin." He draped his arm over mine as he clasped my hand, his fingers soothing my tight fist.

The angle looked awkward; yet, I couldn't push him away.

He watched me as I looked out to the night sky.

"We all have challenges we work through. You're stronger than you think."

"You're kind." I bit my lip staring straight ahead. I dared to face him. "I'm glad you're here," I whispered.

He moved to stand in front of my chair, his hands reaching to me.

I stood up; he took me into his arms. I moved my cheek to the other side. His arms crossed at my neck. His squeeze was firm against the back of my hair. We stood a long time. His chest rose in long breaths against my short and choppy ones. His chin rested near my forehead.

"Let it go."

My shoulders shook; pain fell away.

"Your shirt's wet." I mumbled into his chest.

"What?"

He stepped back slightly, holding my chin in his hand.

I looked up at his eyes and then his lips. "I'm a mess."

He looked down at me. His soft eyes crinkled. He kissed my forehead.

My voice trembled as I tried to talk. I looked down at the ground surrounding our feet. I stepped back. Hot desperate tears fell. He reached toward me, his hands on my shoulders. I shrugged him off and took a deep breath; my chest burned.

"The thing is, —" I looked up at his eyes — "James, I was raped; it was years ago. I've worked through those bad times, tried to let go, but they stay with me, resurfacing at the worst of times."

He reached for me and I let him; his grasp was lighter. "Eva, I'm sorry."

I cried into his chest and stepped away. "The rapes follow me; they're inside. When my doubt and insecurity arise, those bad times define me. And I'm that helpless girl all over again."

He pulled me to him.

When I looked up, his eyes looked red.

"You're not helpless. You're a survivor, a fighter. I told you that before."

I sobbed into his chest and he stroked my back.

I stepped away.

His hand caressed my back. "You fight for your happiness; you're here, aren't you." He said it like an affirmation.

We remained close, his hands resting on the front of my shoulders.

"You remind me of my mum; she never gave up either, always fighting to survive, no matter what the cancer did to her. She would've liked you."

I nodded into his chest. "Thank you," I whispered.

He held me as we stood there in the quiet of the night.

~43~

That night I climbed into bed thinking of James taking me in his arms. I rolled on my side and pulled up the covers over my bare shoulders. Half of my face was buried into the white pillow. A catalogue of memories flooded through me.

Fear crept over me like a shadow. I was sixteen. The door clicked as Jason locked his bedroom door blocking my way out.

Hearing the wind outside blowing through the window slats, I opened my eyes seeing the verdant bush behind my balcony.

Another flash appeared: helping Dad up the steps when he had too much to drink and then blocking it out until that recent call with Mom.

I turned to my other side, patted down the pillow and tried to think of nothing. Another flash came: feeling Michelle had died and having Aunt Patsy confirm it. I opened my eyes to stop the past from returning.

I turned on the light and picked up a novel reading the same paragraph over and over. I turned the light back off and lay face up, staring at the ceiling wondering when I would ever fall asleep.

A memory drifted in. Bill stood above me, laughing at my fright. I kicked away the blankets and stood up. Blood rushed to my head and I held onto the wall for balance. I folded over touching my toes, trying to ground myself. I came back up to standing, looking blankly at the dark wall. I backed up and sat down on the bed and went back under the covers away from the warm spot.

Another flash came: tightness rose in my chest as I forced down feelings of betrayal; Dad's pickup truck around the corner of my street after he took the kitchen table.

I pushed the pillows back behind me and sat up. My hands fell heavily on the bed. I breathed in deeply and let out a long audible exhale blowing out pain that held me captive. My breath continued like this. The racing thoughts stopped and I scrunched down once more under the quilt. The last memory came; James was in front of me and I felt his embrace. I repeated his words in a whisper, "you're a survivor," before closing my eyes.

-44-

When I woke up in the morning, I grabbed my journal and copied the words, writing Dad's letter. I put it in an envelope and scrawled his mailing address. Once at the front desk, I stood holding the white envelope in front of the letter slot. No one was in the office until Suzy walked in and the letter fell out of my hands.

"I took your advice about sending it."

"I'm proud of you."

"I hope it'll be okay."

"It will."

After the practice ended, we had free time; I walked back to my A-Frame. The sun was shining brightly. Freshly showered, I had on my swim suit for the watsu that was starting in a few minutes. A knock sounded at the door.

James stood tall in the frame, his hands in fists at his sides; he squinted his eyes and knitted his eyebrows together.

Before I could ask what's wrong, he spoke, his words in a staccato. "I wasn't sure if you wanted my company. You've kept me at arm's length. I thought it was because I live in Scotland."

"I don't understand. What's wrong? Why are you angry?"

"Why didn't you tell me you're engaged?"

"What? Who told you that?" Fear rushed into my chest. "It wasn't relevant."

"Suzy." James threw his hands up. "I can't believe you could say that."

"No. That's not what I mean. James, Wait a minute — All the wrong words are coming out."

He gave me one last look and walked away taking fast steps.

"James, Please. Don't go." I called after him. "You matter — to me."

He didn't turn. He kept walking. Maybe he didn't hear me.

A wave of sadness rushed through me. I blinked my eyes, taking long breaths to keep my eyes glassy and nothing more.

I looked at the time, three minutes left to get to the watsu area before it started. I took deep breaths as James disappeared from my view. My feet stayed planted. I couldn't make myself move to go after him. My deep breaths came and went; I swallowed away any good feelings I had started to have about love. I shook my head, pretending it didn't matter and looked at the paved trail with each long step to the watsu treatment area.

Mateo and I exchanged greetings.

Shame covered me like a dark shadow. I couldn't meet his eyes.

"Put your clothes over there." He pointed to the white plastic chair. "Then we can begin."

I turned and stepped out of my clothes, folding them on the chair like before. Heat flashed through me. My breath was shallow while I tried to block out any thoughts of James.

"Get in the water." He gestured.

I stood in the middle. Mateo was in my peripheral; I couldn't meet his eyes knowing the hurt I caused James. My gaze focused on the canopy of trees falling down the hillside.

The water moved as he walked closer. "Float on your back, like yesterday, but before you do, imagine doing something you've always wanted. Think of every piece of it, the temperature, the smells, the atmosphere. What are you doing? Who is around you?"

I looked at him to respond, feeling exposed and vulnerable, that I was not a strong person after all. I bit my lip, blinking fast.

He stopped. "Are you alright?"

I nodded.

"Do you want to do this? We don't have to."

I shook my head willing myself not to cry. "I want to — I need to."

He looked at my face. My eyes searched the canopy. Erasing any emotion that might betray me, I looked back at him, taking slow long breaths for a full minute. The breathing forced my emotion down into my stomach and I swallowed hard. My voice was quiet. "I'm okay. Let's do this."

He touched my shoulder and nodded. "Think of this place that's your dream," he started again.

I affirmed and let the place come to me.

"Keep this vision in your mind and float on your back."

I heard the fluttering of water. The wind blew lightly on my exposed skin; palm fronds blew and the birds chirped as my ears came in and out of the water.

"Mmmmm..." He began the one letter chant, the low humming sound. His voice sounded far away when my ears were fully underwater. When my ear dipped out, I heard the monotone letter and birds chirping farther away. One of his hands held my head and his other was holding my legs pinned together.

The scene played out in my mind. I sat outside along a stone walkway in a café in my favorite coastal city, Piran, Slovenia. In front of me was a tall painting stand and a large canvas. Fresh oil paint was on my palette and my brushes lay on the table cloth. I lived intermittently overseas and was in the United States when there was a gallery opening of my latest exhibit. The sun warmed me, as I sat in my sundress on the chair and slid my sandals further under the table.

People talked around me, the high and low hum of accented languages. Shops lined the streets. Cappuccino soothed me. A light breeze blew. I tasted the hot liquid as it slid down my throat and into my belly.

My mind flashed to seeing the jug of red wine on the counter at Dad's new house. That image fell away, and the scene of the coffee shop returned with my paints squeezed on my palette: cadmium red light, yellow ochre, sap green, viridian, cerulean blue, raw sienna, and a big dollop of titanium white.

The blobs of color stayed with me as Mateo swirled and massaged me. Hairs rose on my exposed arms. Though I was aware of my surroundings, my mind was in the café. The image stayed with me like a mantra during meditation.

Mateo's stomach lay against my back. The sound of the swirling water took me away from the sip of my espresso as his hands moved down the sides of my limbs. My body swished like a slow metronome back and forth, and then eventually down under water. My mind drifted back to the cobblestone street, the passing of the sing-song of international voices. While sitting there, I turned and saw James coming toward me. I craned my head looking for him to call out his name but he was gone.

My ear drifted out of the water hearing a bird. The wind blew. The water swished with Mateo's movement away from me.

Peace filled me yet I wasn't sure when it had started.

After the watsu ended, I walked with fast steps back to my room. I changed and ran to James' A-Frame. He wasn't there. I walked to the cafeteria. He sat in the middle of a bunch of others having tea and coffee. I stared right at him but it was as if I didn't exist. Everyone stood up and started walking back to the studio for the next class.

I tried to catch up to James but he avoided me, talking to others. The class started. My muscles remained tense in each pose.

~45~

Class ended.
His back was turned away.

"James!"

He moved his head, his eyes finding mine, his smile fading.

Others left the studio.

"Please —" I reached out.

He stepped away from my grasp. His eyes removed of emotion, looked down at me. "Right. You already said you're engaged. There's not much to add, is there?" He crossed his arms.

We stood alone in the studio.

"I don't know why I hold onto relationships that hurt me."

His eyebrows gathered. "I'm not following."

"I'm trying." I took a breath.

"You're not like the men I'm used to. You caught me off-guard."

"You're taken. I don't see how this changes anything."

"I'm trying to explain."

He remained planted, his arms rigid at his sides.

"Before this trip, my boyfriend — former now — asked

me to get engaged over Email. I never said yes or no. He's already back in Germany. I was supposed to see him; I didn't tell him I'd be coming here."

He stepped back, his hands on his hips. Then he brought them down by his sides.

"You tell yourself it's going to be okay, even when you know it won't be."

"Aye," he almost whispered.

"I've done a lot of hoping in my relationships. Then you come along at one of the worst times in my life. Your kindness brings tears to my eyes. You offer to help me and I haven't even asked. I'm not used to this. I've been letting things happen to me." My voice trembled. I moved my hand across my face.

He didn't speak, nor did he move away.

"No matter what happens — I'm having feelings about you I didn't think I could have. It hasn't been long that we've known each other and part of that feels crazy. My life is a mess. Dealing with my parents' problems and trying to have healthy relationships — well, that hasn't happened. I didn't tell you about Karl because I had doubts for a long time. He wanted me to move to Germany to continue our relationship; getting married was the only way. I had to give up everything. This week I told him on Skype that it's over."

I looked up at James feeling I was blathering on; what I said didn't matter because I'd shut him out. His eyes softened. He remained quiet.

"I'm sorry, James. I knew you were upset. I should've

told you. I tried the other night, but I wanted to enjoy your kindness a little longer. I'm not good at this. I'd never forgive myself if I didn't try to fix this."

He continued looking at me, not saying anything.

I continued with a voice of steel. "Well, I get it. I should've told you. Thanks for listening."

He stared at me like he was looking through me.

"I understand. We're all leaving in a couple days anyway. We'll never see each other again. What's the point, right?" I bit my lip, the words quick and loud out of my mouth. I willed myself not to let him see my eyes filling up. I turned to go toward the door, not wanting to go. The walk felt long. I paused. He didn't call my name; his hand didn't reach for my shoulder. I left the studio not bothering to close the door and walked as fast as I could, putting my hands to my face.

-46-

For the last class Friday afternoon, Doug put on music with a drum beat. The thermometer read 110 degrees.

"I'll call out names and each of you'll have a three minute teaching segment." Doug announced.

James stood on his mat in the back row. I saw him when I came in late, but looked away before he made eye contact.

"Shake your hips to the beat while in the poses."

We went from downward facing dog to forward fold.

"Eva," Doug called out.

I stood up, walking in front of the group.

"Breathe in." I filled up my lungs and then paused. "And out." My breath fell down from my chest to the pit of my belly.

"In your downward dogs, hang your heads. Release any remaining tension." I tipped down someone's neck and gave a massage on the back of her head.

"Give this practice to yourself. You've earned it." I walked in the middle of all the students, projecting my voice, turning my head to look at everyone.

James met my eyes.

I looked away from him letting the sea of hopeful

faces be my focus. "Crescent lunge on your right. Right foot forward. Feel that stretch, like your legs are one long line. Class, you look fabulous! Twist to your right." I continued teaching and walked around the room and across the front.

Bright eyes greeted me. David and Liz looked up, smiles dancing in their eyes.

"Good, everyone. You're doing great."

"Liz..." Doug called out. I raced back to my mat, positioning myself into crescent lunge.

After the last class, the students' voices were high pitched mixed in with the sea of laughter. Some high-fived each other.

James approached me. "Brilliant!" He made a thumbs up sign.

I glanced at the crowd trying to figure out where I could blend in. I looked up as he came closer. "Thanks." I backed away.

He walked toward me, his hands reaching to me.

I saw Suzy, took a deep breath and turned away as far from James as I could.

For the evening exercise, we formed a circle. James stood next to me; I couldn't avoid him this time. When forming the circle, he took my hand with a warm and firm grip. The circle bent so each person was looking into the eyes of every other before moving on. James looked at me, embraced me and kissed my cheek. He paused, looking in my eyes. I tried not to melt into him, stepped away and swallowed a big lump in my throat pushing down the sadness of what wouldn't be. We both moved on to the next person in line. I felt his eyes follow me but I couldn't look back.

After dinner during the bonfire, drums evoked dancing. I took pictures of those shaking hips with the tambourine moving around the fire. I stood to the side watching the fire throwers juggling. The flames whipped up and down in the night; bright stars shined above. James wasn't in the crowd. I smiled at others, stayed a while and eventually went back to my room.

-47-

In the early morning, I did a yoga practice by the watsu area on the side of the hot tub. I moved into pigeon pose, stretching my leg in the air and brought it forward. My hips settled into the mat. Certainty filled me as I thought about having mailed the letter to Dad. My arms stretched ahead of me, my forehead resting on my mat. Birds chirped. Below was the green hillside that had become a comfort of familiarity.

I felt a sensation of being watched. I turned around.

James watched me, having sat cross-legged on his mat behind me.

"How long have you been sitting there?" I called out, turning.

"Long enough." A flicker of a smile appeared.

I didn't return it. "You don't have to do this." I leaned down and started gathering my things to leave. I paused looking at the greenery we had looked at so much together from the balcony. My breath felt jagged and I shook my head, blinked and looked for an easy path away; I'd have to walk past him to get to the steps. I turned.

He blocked my path, standing in front of me.

I moved to walk around him. "Please don't make this awkward," my voice cracked; my tears followed. "After today we won't see each other again." I looked down at the pavement around the jacuzzi.

His hand clipped my chin. "Will you look at me?"

I shook my head. "Please don't do this. I'm trying to leave."

"Don't."

"Don't what?" The tears came down my cheeks.

"Don't go. You had your chance to talk. I didn't. You left before I could answer."

"Your lack of response said it all." I bit back.

His hand dropped away from my chin.

My feet were like cement. I stared at a green bush behind him. I breathed in and ignored my tears. I sniffed and wiped my forearm across my face.

His arms wrapped around me. I felt his chest move against mine. I didn't struggle to get away. His arms were tight against the back of my hair. I sobbed. I hated that I was showing him all this.

He held me, readjusting his stance.

After my sounds quieted, he moved. "Eva, look up."

I studied his eyes, the familiar crinkles in the corners. I sniffed; my arms lifeless around him. They fell to my sides. I tried to look away but couldn't.

I pulled away and stared at the ground. "We're leaving tomorrow. I have to forget about us to move on." I picked up my mat and the blocks to walk away. As I stood up again, his hand reached for my shoulder. "Wait," his voice broke.

I didn't move.

"Listen to me. You had your chance to say what you needed. I didn't and you left."

My jaw ached.

"When Suzy said you were engaged, I felt like you were playing me."

"That's not true."

"Then you said your engagement wasn't relevant. I thought you didn't care. I didn't want to believe that. I couldn't."

"No, that wasn't it." Fatigue fell over me like a familiar shadow.

"I—," James paused.

I stood in front of him knowing I would not move away.

"I wouldn't have felt hurt if I didn't care."

"James, I'm sorry. I didn't expected any of this to happen—"

He brought me inside his arms.

I broke away from him. "You listened and — I never thought anything, you — this good could come to me."

He took my chin in my hands and kissed me. He pulled away, our eyes unwavering. We stood like this awhile.

"Let's sit on the balcony. It's our place."

I nodded.

He took my hand and we walked together, not saying anything.

We settled in the chairs as he moved closer. He slid his feet out of his sandals and put them up on the railing. I did the same.

I didn't continue where he left off. "James, you never said why you came to this retreat."

He was quiet as the birds chirped and cars wove up a street far below our resort.

"I haven't started dating anyone in the year since my divorce. Fiona was an only child; she was nothing like my mother. Mum always fought until the end. When you told me about the things that happened to you, it showed me your will to fight. I want to be with you. I haven't felt like that with anyone in a long time. No one else has interested me until you."

Chills rose on my arms and I pulled my knees and face into my chest.

I felt his eyes on me; I couldn't believe what he might be saying.

I pulled my legs away, putting my feet on the ground and dared to see his face.

Kindness filled his eyes, the smile returned to his mouth. "You gave me courage to contact my dad. We hadn't been in touch, not since my mother's death. He's in a nursing home. My younger brother visits; he's kept me updated and I've talked to his doctors to make sure he's getting the best care. But I haven't seen or talked to my dad in years. You gave me the strength to call him. We talked the other night."

"You did that yourself. I didn't do anything."

"Listening to you helped me more than you know, Eva."

I gave a slight nod. "How'd it go?"

"Dad cracked the same jokes he used to. We laughed a lot."

"Good." I paused.

He was quiet. "I wish you could've met her, — my mum." He turned toward me. "I felt your losses as if they were my own."

I breathed in.

"Eva. We can do this."

Heat rose inside me. I looked at him, not knowing what to say, not willing myself to accept the idea of — us.

He put his hand over mine.

I didn't move it away. "Why did you come to this retreat?"

"To help others and to further develop spiritually and physically."

I nodded.

"And what about you, Eva?"

I answered his question without thinking. "To be open to love and light. What came later was knowing I can control what happens in my life. I even thought I could find healthy love."

"And what about now?" He stood up, his hands out to mine.

I took them not knowing what was next.

We stood close. I searched his face. He leaned down to me; intertwining my hands with his, now hanging at our sides.

I smiled looking up at him. "Thank you." I whispered. The wall I'd worked hard to keep around me crumbled. The tension from my neck and shoulders disappeared. Audibly, I breathed out. I looked at him again, this time studying the lines on his mouth.

Our lips touched, soft, hovering, drifting toward each other.

Warm, soothing energy moved through me like streams of light that had not penetrated before.

He put his hands on my cheeks. "Eva, you're the woman I was hoping for."

He tucked a stray piece of hair behind my ear. "I admire your courage, not that I'll let you forget."

As our lips met, my eyes blinked tears of joy. He wiped them away; we shared a soft laugh and delighted in each other.

Acknowledgements

Sincere thanks goes to my editor, Rachel Weaver at Sandstone Editing. This book would not be what it is today without her keen insight in structure, character development and plot lines.

Thank you to my family and friends for supporting and loving me as I've worked to make this dream possible. Lastly, thank you, readers, for buying my book and reading Eva's story about living life as an adult child of an alcoholic.

Amanda L. Mottorn, Author/Artist
Connect with me!
Facebook: https://www.facebook.com/amanda.mWriter
Instagram: @amandamottornartistwriter
Twitter: @EpistemicSeeker
Blog page: https://amlindsayblog.wordpress.com

Websites:
https://society6.com/outdoortraveler4169
https://shopvida.com/collections/amanda-mottorn

Made in the USA
Middletown, DE
12 March 2021

34645290R00182